DEATH

RIDES A

BOBCAT

The Possumwood Mysteries Book 5

HOLLY DEY

Death Rides a Bobcat: The Possumwood Mysteries Book 5 ©
2022 by Holly Dey. All rights reserved.

Black Mare Books

First Edition 2022

This is a work of fiction. Names, characters, places, brands, media, and incidents are either the product of the author's imagination or are used fictitiously. The author acknowledges the trademarked status and trademark owners of various products referenced in this work of fiction, which have been used without permission. The publication/use of these trademarks is not authorized, associated with, or sponsored by the trademark owners.

ISBN: 978-1-941502-23-5

Acknowledgements

I couldn't do this without the love and support of my wonderful family. I love you so much!

Chapter 1

RETIRED DETECTIVE SERGEANT PC Donovan lay on her back on the concrete. It was utterly dark, and she couldn't tell if the moisture soaking her clothes was sweat or humidity. Something metal skidded across the cement, but she didn't dare move—the floor of the flatbed trailer was inches from her face. She gripped the steel handle in her right hand, making sure the business end was pointed away from her.

The back door opened, and the brighter darkness of the starlit May night poured in for a moment before it shut again.

A small but intense light tore through the gloom. She saw it moving in her direction, and she started to slide carefully away from the wheel of the flatbed trailer.

"Power's out everywhere."

Drew Burlesconi set his cell phone on the Maifest parade float and helped her up from the floor. She dusted herself off.

"We're so close to being done," she said, setting down the upholstery stapler. "Wonder what caused it?"

"No telling. But without the fan, this garage is stifling. Let's get some air." He stooped to pick up the pliers he'd kicked in the dark.

"Agreed. We still have tomorrow to finish up, but if I never have to make a giant tissue paper rose again, I'm completely fine with that."

Drew chuckled and shined the light on the six-foot tall, 3D version of Renoir's *Spring Bouquet*, composed mostly of tissue paper flowers and fabric leaves. The elegant Delft Blue pottery vase was papier mâché molded over a trash can.

He turned the light toward the door, and they exited the garage into his tidy brick courtyard. The fountain was lit up with blue and white lights, so the water that poured from the bronze boy's pitcher was a sparkling cyan. It felt very European to PC, although she'd only ever been to London once for a conference.

Drew opened the back door. "Glass of wine?"

PC looked at her FlitBit, the knock-off fitness tracker her sister had gotten her as a retirement gift. She had to tap the display a couple of times to make it come on. Finally, it lit up with the time and her step count.

"It's after ten already. I'm sure nobody's taken Cordite out to pee. Poor guy, he's probably waiting at the door with his legs crossed."

"You should get a doggie door put in for him."

"And have him out in the yard barking at Mama's 'possums all night? No, thanks. That's if he made it past the giant semi-feral cats that live on her back porch. Three of 'em are about as big as he is, and any one of them could shred him like a wood chipper. But the four of them together?" PC grimaced and shook her head.

"What, like Pestilence, War, Famine, and Death?"

"Could be an apocalypse for Cordie. Anyway, give me a shout tomorrow when you're ready to finish up that canopy."

"We could get dinner first. *Truffles!*, maybe?"

PC had been doing some contract work for the Possumwood Police Department, but she was still trying to go easy on her cash, and she refused to let him pay. "How about the *Brisk Rib*? I can get a plate for Mama and Rocky while we're there."

"Sure. The gallery closes at 6:00, so 6:30?"

"See you then."

PC walked out the front door to her SUV that was parked in the street. Drew stood between the pillars of his Greek Revival home, presumably watching to make sure she got safely on the road. She started the car and waved, but wasn't sure he saw her in the dark.

When she got to her mother's house, her terrier-mix dog, Cordite, started yapping and scratching at the door as soon as she set foot on the walkway.

"*Shhhh.* Let's not wake the entire household, okay?"

She opened the door, and he bounded out, dancing at her feet for a few moments before running into the grass to find his favorite tree. When they came back in the house, she noticed the living room lights were on, and so was the TV.

"Rocky? You're up late."

Her brother sprawled on the couch, and for a terrible moment, PC was afraid he'd been drinking.

"Yeah. Having trouble sleeping."

"Everything okay?"

He moved to face her. "I'm sure Mama told you about Kyle."

PC sat in the recliner, and Cordite jumped into her lap, trying to lick her face. She put up her hand to avoid being drowned in dog slobber. "She said you were working with him through a program at the Methodist church, and he wanted you to be his sponsor."

"Yeah. Well, he hasn't been to the last four Tuesday night meetings, or church either, for that matter. I got him some new clothes, well, new to him, anyway, so he'd have something nice to wear."

"I'm sorry, Rocky. Some people don't want to be saved. You can throw them a lifeline, but you can't make them grab it."

"I know that," he snapped. "But Kyle…he wanted to get clean. Mama said he was a drifter, and just drifted to the next town, but I didn't want to believe that."

"So, what's changed?"

"I got a letter from him today." He handed PC an envelope. It was postmarked from San Angelo.

She took out the letter and read it.

Dear Rocky:

Bruther, I really apreesheate everything you tried to do for me. But that liddel town. Not for me. I'm headed to Midland to get a good payan job in the oil patch. Done some ruffneckin before. Stay kool.

Kyle

"Well, at least he let you know he wasn't dead in a ditch somewhere." She tucked the letter back into its envelope and handed it to him.

"There's that, I guess. I just really thought I'd got through to him." Rocky frowned at the paper. "You'd think somebody with a master's degree would be a better speller."

"Sorry, Rock. People aren't always who we think they are."

"Ain't that the truth."

PC ruffled Cordite's beard, scratching him on the chin. "I bought some ice cream yesterday. You up for any?"

"Fudge sauce?"

"And butterscotch."

PC pushed the shaggy donkey, Guinevere, off of her foot. "You did that on purpose, didn't you?"

Gwen looked around, eyes wide with innocence as her radar dish ears swiveled forward.

"I'm sorry I'm late. You are in no danger of starving to death, you little chonky donkey."

One ear flicked back at the insult.

Mmmmaaa! Maamaaaa! Hazel, the three-legged goat, inserted herself into the conversation.

Arthur stood with his head twisted at an awkward angle so that he could see what was going on. The handsome Catalan jack was missing his left eye, so PC always had to make sure she was on his right. If she startled him, Gwen would come after her.

PC retrieved three small pails, one for each critter, from the feed room and emptied the buckets into the appropriate rubber feed tubs. Then she got a scoop of hen scratch and spread it in the dirt around the chicken coop before letting Pavarotti and his hens out for the morning. As soon as the door opened, they ran out like they were going to a Black Friday sale with a fist full of coupons.

Cordite sat panting on the back steps, past ready to go inside and sit in the air conditioning.

A black truck pulled up alongside the fence, then backed into the short driveway that provided access to the livestock pen from the road. The diesel engine clattered to a halt, startling the animals. But not enough to leave their feed.

Justice Johnson got out and opened the gate. It was almost exactly as wide as her truck, with seemingly no room for Houdini quadrupeds, but she was well aware that Gwen was an experienced escapologist, so she closed it behind her. As always, Justice wore jeans and a denim shirt. A blue baseball cap covered grey hair that was cropped even shorter than PC's.

"Mornin', Justice. You're here early."

She glanced at the tarp that covered the bed of her truck. "Yup. I was gonna go in and have a cup of coffee with your mama 'fore I got started. Then I have an interview 'round lunchtime with that Dr. McIlwraith."

"The state archaeologist?"

"Yeah, yeah. He's got some kinda dig goin' on at the mayor's house. Poor ole Phineas Scott don't know what hit him. Most of the back yard is gridded off with strings—looks like they're getting' ready to pour a concrete slab."

"I was talking to Phineas the other day. He said McIlwraith's pretty convinced that skeleton they found in his old well was Francois de Lamartine. I was surprised they were able to get a viable DNA sample after almost two hundred years."

When he disappeared in 1860, who would have ever guessed that the trail might lead to the bottom of his own well?

"They're testin' it against Lamartine's descendants to see if there's a match." Justice rubbed her cheek. "I haven't heard anything back yet. My mouth is just now getting back to bein' right."

"You got a DNA swab? I hadn't realized you were related to Lamartine."

"Yup. He married the eldest daughter of Zachariah and Ruth Justice. That's where I get my name."

"Of course. What's he going to interview you about? Did he tell you?"

"Dr. McIlwraith told me to bring the family bible, if we had one. The old-fashioned kind with weddin's and births and whatnot written in it. I know there's one around somewhere, but I haven't been able to find it. I think it may be in a trunk in the attic, but I ain't had time to go up and dig around. He said he's goin' out of town for the weekend, then he's takin' a week's vacation—don't wanna get caught up in all the Maifest hubbub. Goin' hikin' at Big Bend instead."

"Yeah, I guess being downtown would put him at ground zero. Well, let's go in and get you that coffee."

PC left Justice in the kitchen with her mother, Rose, and retired to her room. She'd been spending her evenings over at Drew's for the past week and a half, working on that crazy Maifest float. Guilt clawed at her insides—she had only picked up Trey Donovan's murder book once in that time. Her father's killing forty years ago remained unsolved, and she was hoping that by going over every piece of evidence, she could glean some clue, no matter how small. Now, she felt like she'd let him down by letting the binder just sit and collect dust.

After an hour and a half of re-reading reports, she was no closer to finding a clue than she had been when she came back to Possumwood in January to take care of her mother after her hip replacement. She got in the shower—no point in smelling like the stockyards when she and Drew met at the Brisk Rib for barbecue later.

What is that noise? A radio? That's a terrible song. Then she realized it was her 5:45 alarm. She had to get the animals fed, take a shower, put on her costume and be at Drew's by 7:00 AM so they could line up for the parade and get a good spot. Wilma Gatewood, the acrylics teacher who worked part time at Drew's art gallery, would meet them there. She and PC would sit under the silk flower-festooned canopy and wave regally while Drew drove the truck. Check-in started at 8:30, and no one wanted to be late for that. While Possumwood PD took a dim view of people lining up overnight, a few (fool)hardy souls showed up around 6 AM. Drew wasn't obsessed with being first, but he didn't want to be last in line, either. By then, the heat would be setting in, and the judges would be pig-sick of looking at floats.

PC got her chores done and arrived at his house at 6:58. Drew met her in the driveway, a travel mug of coffee in hand.

"You look great. Green really suits you. Brings out the color of your eyes."

It's not my eyes you're looking at, though. PC tugged at her mid-thigh length skirt as she felt heat rise in her face. "Thanks."

He clicked a button on his remote and the garage door started opening. A frenzy of motion inside caught PC off guard. Then she saw a dark grey rat disappear behind a trash bin.

The color drained from Drew's face, and PC's mouth fell open.

Chapter 2

A HOLE THE size of a large man's fist gaped in the papier mâché
vase, exposing the trash can behind the facade. Rats apparently
had started snacking on it as soon as Drew and PC left the garage
around midnight.

"What are we going to do?" PC crossed her arms.

"We can't put more papier mâché on it—it'll never dry in time,
and probably just fall off." Drew looked around the garage franti-
cally. "Paper towels!"

He ran through the garage to the back door of the house.

Shaking her head, PC moved closer to survey the damage.
Could they spray paint the garbage bin, so it was less noticeable?

Drew came running back with three paper towels folded on top
of each other. He thrust the towels and a blue Sharpie marker into
PC's hands. "Draw the missing vase design on the paper towels."

"I'm not sure—"

"Just do it. It's abstract—you'll be fine. I've got to find
that spackle."

PC did her best to make some random lines on the towels that
more or less matched the random lines on the vase. She held it over
the hole to see if she needed any touch-ups.

"Perfect!" Drew all but shoved her out of the way and started
smearing spackle on the edges of the paper towels to stick them to
the faux vase. From a distance, she could hardly tell.

Drew slapped the lid back on the can. "I'm going to back up the truck."

He hurried to his SUV. To his credit, he backed up very carefully, almost perfectly in line with the trailer tongue. He jumped out and quickly closed the hitch, applied the chain, plugged in the lights, then threw up his hands like a calf roper does to stop the timer.

"Let's roll."

PC texted Wilma to tell her they were running a little late, but she did not mention why. Probably, the fewer people who knew, the better.

They arrived later than they thought, ending up in the dreaded last place slot, Drew's least desired location.

He had to help both PC and Wilma climb up into the float. They wore snug green sequin cocktail dresses with hats that looked like large daisies. PC rarely wore dresses, and she kept tugging the skirt down toward her knees. Luckily, Drew had put the stepstool in the truck the night before to make it easier for them to step up and board the float. The women sat on their plastic-garland-covered thrones, waiting for the parade officials to come trade Drew's entry form for a large paper number, which he'd tape on the door of the truck.

The detective took in the chaos surrounding her. Float riders made emergency costume adjustments or received last-minute props. One child in a group of small children dressed as fairies began to wail. Like dominoes, the others fell into line and joined her. Harried moms tried to coax them into silence. That only made things worse. PC didn't envy them.

She jerked her gaze away, in the vain hope that not looking at the toddlers would somehow make their caterwauling cease. Her eyes fell on the mouth of an alley. A tall man stood at the edge of it, a white plastic garbage bag dangling from one hand. Judging by his filthy, mismatched clothes, he was homeless. He peered at PC from under a stained ball cap, and that searing look gave her the willies. He turned back into the alley and was gone, the bag rattling at his side as he walked away. She wrenched her attention back to the steamy parade float.

PC was glad of the light breeze. Even in the shade of the canopy, she had started to sweat, which made the sequined fabric itchy. It took a lot of control not to scratch at her armpits, where the dress was a little tight.

A scampering noise came from the giant vase. PC held her breath. *Rodent stowaways. Great.*

Wilma looked around. "Did you hear something?"

"I'm sure it's just the wind."

One corner of Wilma's mouth turned down. "Doesn't sound much like wind to me, but…" She shrugged.

The vase quieted down. Finally, the officials stopped by with their number. PC and Wilma each made a regal queen's parade wave while smiling benevolently.

As Drew taped the number on the truck's door, scratching came from the vase. PC faked an extended cough. The noise stopped. Wilma didn't seem to notice. She was taking pictures of the sky and other random subjects with her cell phone. *Artists. Go figure.* PC tried to read a book on her own phone, but she kept looking at the vase, as if her hard stare would keep the rats trapped inside calm and still.

At long last, the parade got started. The float lurched into motion and the ladies very nearly slid off their fabric-covered plywood thrones. But they smiled and waved like Queen Elizabeth.

By the time they made the turn to approach the judges' stand, PC's cheeks ached. They were almost through the parade, and no catastrophes. It would be funny when it was all over. The parade stopped for a group of twirlers to perform in front of the judges.

PC spotted her mother and sibs under an oak tree not far from the platform. They waved to her, and she gave them a real wave, a momentary slip before she slid back into the parade queen skin.

The twirlers' music stopped, applause followed, and they bowed. The parade moved on. Just before the truck pulled even with the judge's platform, Vivaldi's *Spring* concerto began to blast from a hidden speaker in the vase.

The scuffling started again.

Then became frantic.

PC watched the judges' faces morph from cheer to horror as rats began to burst out of the paper towel quick fix on the vase. Rats panicked and squealed, leaping off the float onto the onlookers. Onlookers panicked and squealed, knocking each other down in their desperation to flee. Wilma fainted.

PC looked for her family. Rocky had moved Rose's wheelchair behind the tree, which acted as a watershed against the churning crowd. She could only see some of her brother's back, and her mother's lower legs. But Daisy leaned out from behind the trunk and glared right at her.

Wilma was fine. They dropped her off at the staging area, and she wobbled across the parking lot to the vendor booths to man *The Best Little Art Gallery in Texas'* table. Who knew she had musophobia?

Once they were alone, PC turned to Drew. He looked like a dog caught rummaging through the trash.

PC began to laugh. She couldn't stop, not until tears ran down her face. Her stomach hurt, and she could hardly breathe. It was like a dam somewhere inside had broken.

When she could finally speak, she said, "That was probably the most entertaining parade I've ever seen."

Drew snorted, then drove them back to his place. He left the float sitting in the driveway and parked the large SUV next to it. The red tail hawks sitting on the power lines would keep any varmints at bay for the rest of the afternoon.

PC changed into her normal clothes—a polo and slacks—and they walked the three blocks from Drew's house to the dual town squares. There was one around the county courthouse on the west side and another around City Hall on the east side. A large park, straight out of a Norman Rockwell painting, lay in between them. The roads were closed around both squares, and various arts, crafts, and food vendors took up all of the parking areas for the city green and most of the blocked-off streets. Bands took turns playing in the oversized gazebo in the middle of the park.

PC and Drew garnered a few dirty looks from random people in the crowd. Thankfully, their float had only been followed by a small group of trail riders, and no one felt strongly enough about the parade being cut short by five minutes to confront them about it. A few whispered and snickered. Arguably, that was worse.

An old brick tower stood at the center front of the park. Something to do with a nineteenth-century sewer or cistern, but PC wasn't sure if she had ever known the details. In the time since she had left home, a small sign for *Wings Over Possumwood* had sprung up in front of it.

Drew nudged her. "The bats should come out around dusk. I think there's a bat talk that starts around 7:30, but they won't let the bands play while the bats are emerging."

Rocky took Rose home around six. PC had given him detailed feeding instructions for the menagerie. She hoped he'd follow them.

Daisy stayed. PC's feet hurt, and she ached to sit for a while, but her sister was having none of it. She was raring to hit the Biersal Brew Pub beer tent now that Rose and Rocky had gone home.

Drew planned to work the last hour and a half of sales so Wilma could get something to eat and do a little shopping.

"We'll meet you back here before *Deutsche Boyz* go on at eight," PC called to him as Daisy led her away.

Once she had a persimmon ale in hand, Daisy flitted from jewelry booth to jewelry booth. PC got the last apricot kolache from the *Czech Mate* table. They also had klobasneks, which people not in the know called 'sausage kolaches,' but they were too spicy for her taste. PC admired some stained-glass art pieces, and when she looked around, she saw her sister being chatted up by a man somewhat her junior.

Daisy was an incorrigible flirt. Perhaps it came from being a middle child. While she did date and spend a fair number of Saturday evenings down at the Silver Dollar Saloon, she was waiting until both of her boys were out of the house before she got serious about anybody. She dressed for attention, but never accepted any of the inevitable offers or invitations.

They ran into a group of thirty or forty people, standing in a loose circle around the brick tower near the edge of the park.

"What—"

Shhhhh! A man glared at PC.

The detective recoiled, startled and slightly annoyed at being shushed by a stranger. Heads in front of her rotated upward, and PC followed the motion. Bats had begun to fly out of the tower. Within minutes, the trickle turned into a river as hundreds of bats fluttered into the sky in search of insects.

The stream of bats thinned and stopped. A young woman in a purple shirt with a bright yellow bat embroidered on the left side of her chest raised an arm and waved. "The bats have left the building. Let the concert begin."

PC looked at her FlitBit, then tapped her sister, who was whispering with the young man, on the shoulder. "Time to go meet Drew."

Daisy and her suitor followed a few feet behind her, gabbing away. When they got to the gallery's tent, Drew was packing up. He had some large locking bins that he was carefully placing his wares in.

Daisy batted her eyelashes. "This is Slade. He's from Horice. Works at the auto parts store."

PC nodded at him.

"Nice to meet you, Slade," Drew said, still packing his boxes. Once he was done, he covered the bins in a tarp and tucked the ends under the containers.

"I don't think it's supposed to rain tonight, but you never know. Did anybody bring a blanket?" He looked around. "No? Maybe we can find a bench."

"I'm really tired." PC yawned.

"We can't leave without hearing the band! They came all the way from Dallas." Daisy pouted.

PC sighed. She could get a killer to confess, almost every time, but she couldn't talk sense into her little sister. Probably because she wouldn't be stuck in the car with a killer whining at her or calling to complain the rest of the week.

"Thirty minutes."

Daisy drooped. "Fine."

They found a single bench, far from the bandstand. Most people sat on blankets on the grass all around the gazebo. Drew and Slade bookended PC and Daisy, who were crammed together in the middle.

The band started to play. They had fused classic German oompah with various other genres, like rap, metal, and reggae. Some of it wasn't too bad. Some of it sounded like a bunch of angry cats tied up in a wet burlap sack.

PC struggled to keep her eyes open. Her chin seemed to be magnetized to her chest. One minute, the lead singer was screaming about beer barrels. The next, someone was shaking her awake. She found that she'd fallen asleep, and her neck was stiff from resting it on Drew's shoulder. The band had left the gazebo, and people were rolling up their blankets.

"You weren't lying when you said you were tired." Drew shook out the arm she'd been leaning against and smiled at her.

"Sorry about that."

Daisy and Slade were standing at the other end of the bench, talking.

PC stood and stretched her back and neck. It would be sore for a while. "Let's go, Daisy. I'm parked at Drew's."

"I can give you a lift," Slade piped up, hope in his voice.

"Thank you for your kind offer. But not tonight." Daisy's tone hinted that there might be another night, just not this one. She stood on her toes and gave him the tiniest peck on the cheek, then left him standing all alone.

Once they got to Drew's house, PC fished her car keys out of her bag and unlocked the doors with her remote.

"'Night, Drew." Daisy waved as she got in the compact SUV.

He waved back.

PC squirmed. "I'm sorry I used you as a pillow."

"I'm not."

Heat raced to her cheeks, and she was glad it was dark. "Um... well, I. I've got to get Daisy home. I'll see you later."

"Good night."

He watched from the front gate as they drove away.

Daisy snickered.

"What?"

"You snore."

"No, I don't." PC hit the brakes a little too hard at the stop sign.

"Oh, yes, you do." Daisy giggled again.

"At least I wasn't stringing some hapless man along," PC snapped.

"At least I'm not afraid to admit I have feelings," Daisy shot back. "What do you think you're doin' with Drew? It's so obvious that he has the hots for you."

"That is between me and him, and none of *your* business." PC slowed to turn a corner. "Daisy, please. Don't be such a tease with these random men, okay?"

"Speaking as my holier-than-thou older sister?" Daisy snarled.

"Speaking as a homicide detective."

They drove the rest of the way to Daisy's house in silence.

Sunday morning was overcast and muggy. PC's clothes were damp, and she was ready to be done mucking the pen. On the bright side, they'd gotten through the Maifest main event without a body turning up. That was something right there. Was the streak broken?

She put the manure fork away and gave Gwen, who had been closely scrutinizing PC's scooping technique, a scratch on the head before heading for the gate.

Had Rocky gathered the eggs last night? She should probably check.

Rose stood on the back porch, cell phone in hand.

"Primrose!"

"What is it, Mama?"

"Can you get over to Justice's? She's half out of her mind! There's a skeleton in her compost."

Chapter 3

"THERE'S A *WHAT* in her compost?" PC wasn't sure she heard what she thought she heard.

"Oh, honey. You heard what I said. A skeleton. Bones. Those white sticks under your skin?" Rose pursed her lips.

PC stepped up onto the back porch. "I know what a skeleton is, Mama. Has she called the Possumwood Police Department? Dr. McIlwraith? If it's skeletonized remains… how old is her compost pile, anyway?"

Rose hobbled into the house, her cane nowhere in sight. "She did call the po-lice. Thorne Marberger's cows are out, all 250 of 'em, and they're blockin' 720. Traffic's already backed up into downtown from people tryin' to get back home after Maifest. The cop told her if it was just bones, it wasn't an emergency, but they'd be out once the cattle were wrangled. Can you *please* go and see about it?"

"Fine, Mama. May not be much I can do, but if it'll make you feel better…"

PC took the long way around to avoid the traffic and the cows on the way to Justice's place. She pulled into the gravel drive, wincing each time the tires threw up a rock that hit the car. Up ahead, a custom wrought-iron arch said 'Capre Leche Farm.' Beneath it, metal silhouettes of goats capered about the two panels of the matching gate. Fortunately, it was open. PC waved at the security camera as she drove through. Justice's three dogs, a small beaglesque pupper; a medium eclectic mix of breeds; and a large shaggy grey doggo trotted out to sound the alarm and inspect her car.

Justice met her in front of the house. "Glad you could make it. Let me put the dogs up before we go down there. Don't want 'em chewin' on the po-lice."

The dogs reluctantly followed Justice's whistle and slunk into a large pen with a huge custom doghouse in the middle of it. There was room for all three of them and a few of their closest friends in there.

PC slid out of her SUV. "Mama says there's a skeleton in your compost. Tell me about it."

Justice led the way toward some outbuildings. "I had a pile of well-rotted manure that was ready to go. I used the Bobcat to scoop it up and take it to the mushroom bunker. When I dumped the load, there it was."

They covered the remaining distance to the underground building, and sure enough, there was a skeleton partially buried in the crumbly compost. The yellowed bones didn't look fresh. There were no visible fabric scraps to indicate clothing.

PC knew from a quarter-century of experience that a body lying on the ground in the Texas summer could be skeletonized in a week, but they were also prone to being scavenged. Animals would scatter the bones near and far. A buried body could take a year or more, depending on the substrate. From what she could see, this one had at least most of its parts, so it had most likely been buried.

"Well." PC ran a hand through her salt and pepper hair. "My best guess is that this individual was placed in a shallow grave, at least a year ago, and you just happened to make your pile there. When you scooped it up with the loader, you got the grave and skeleton, too."

Justice's eyes narrowed. "Why don't you come have a look at my pile."

PC followed her. "If Possumwood PD doesn't, I think you ought to call Dr. DuPree. Bones are her specialty."

"I probably still have her card from when they did the DNA sample."

They reached the piles of decomposing manure. Justice pointed to one area. The soil was dark with compost. PC could see markings where the loader scraped across the dirt. There was no evidence of a clandestine grave. But what else could it be? PC was reasonably sure she hadn't left any skeletons lying around the manure pile at Rose's house.

"Do you get your poop from anybody except Mama?"

"I get a fair amount from the horse farm."

"Is it loaded in bulk, like from a Bobcat, or do you hand shovel it into bags, like at Mama's? I guess what I mean is, would you have noticed if there was a skeleton in the manure you got from them?"

Justice cocked her head. "What kind of question is that? Of course, I would have."

"Why don't you call Dr. DuPree and tell her what's going on? Don't know if PPD has had time to get in contact, given their current roundup extravaganza, but she needs to be called, regardless. In the meantime, you got a tarp we can cover up those bones with?"

PC took the deluxe self-guided tour of the mushroom bunker while Justice called the anthropologist. It was a rectangular concrete room, about ten feet wide by twenty feet long. A couple of hanging light fixtures lit up the space with a dim yellow glow. White mushrooms bubbled out of growing tables filled with dark, rich compost. It wasn't quite as cool as a cave, but the temperature was very comfortable. PC climbed the stairs back to the surface.

Justice was still on her phone. "…yup…yeah, yeah…No, we'll be here."

"She's able to come out?"

"Yup. She's at College Station, just finishin' up a workshop. Be here in twenty, thirty minutes."

PC leaned against the Bobcat. "How did your interview with Dr. McIlwraith go?"

"Fine, fine. Never did find that family Bible he asked for, though. Told him I'd keep lookin' for it."

PC nodded. She wasn't often with Justice when Rose wasn't nearby. *Seems like a golden opportunity.* "So, uh, what do you think of Terry Gillespie?"

"Rose's boyfriend?"

"Yeah."

Justice sucked her teeth. "He's alright. Too flashy for my taste. But he sure is fond of your mama."

"The feeling seems to be mutual. But…"

"Trey Donovan was a good man, and he loved your mama like nobody's business. But he's been gone a long time. It's no disrespect to him if she falls in love again."

PC sighed. "I know. At least in my head, anyway."

"Come with me." Justice started back towards the farmhouse.

PC tagged along until they got to a goat pen. Justice opened the gate and motioned PC inside. Once the gate was closed behind them, Justice whistled. Nanny goats came trotting up, full udders swinging. Goat kids leaped in the air and then sprang on all four legs at once like miniature antelopes. Justice waded into the flock and picked up a small white goat, then handed her to PC. The goat bleated, and PC scratched her neck. She seemed to enjoy it and rested her head on PC's shoulder.

Justice grinned. "Nothing cures a bad mood like baby goats."

PC chuckled and set the kid down. The goat ran off to play chase with the others. They ran circles around a large white donkey and a smaller one that looked a lot like Guinevere.

"Is there a law in Possumwood that requires you to own a donkey if you have at least one goat?" PC brushed some white hair off her shirt.

Justice laughed. "Nope. But you'll have 'em if you wanna keep the coyotes away from your livestock."

PC's forehead crinkled. "Why's that?"

"Donkeys and coyotes are mortal enemies. Donkeys, especially the jennies, won't tolerate a coyote on the place, and the 'yotes are smart enough to steer clear. Haven't lost a single goat since I got Christine and Jelly."

The two women watched the kids cavorting around the stoic equids until Dr. DuPree arrived.

She got out of her truck. "Morning, ladies. I tell you, the stars must be aligned just so for you guys to have uncovered two antique skeletons in less than a month."

"Not sure about antique," PC said. "But the bones are kind of yellowy-brown, so they don't look too recent."

"Let's have a look." DuPree slung a backpack over her shoulders.

Justice led the way to the bunker, then she and PC removed the tarp. DuPree snapped on some nitrile gloves and squatted to examine the bones. Her brow furrowed. She lifted one of the arms.

"Whoa!"

"What's wrong?" PC craned her neck to see the skeleton.

"These bones are not old. They're very fresh, actually."

Chapter 4

"WHAT?" PC AND Justice said together.

Dr. DuPree stood up. "The bones are way too heavy to be as old as they look." She leaned over and rotated the closest arm. "Look at this!" She pointed to the underside of the humerus. "That is a drip mark. These bones have been treated with some kind of paint or dye."

"Who in blazes would do that?" Justice pulled her cap off and shook her head.

DuPree squatted again and inspected the shoulders and skull. "Definitely tool marks here. Someone went to a whole lot of trouble to disguise this..." she looked at the pelvis. "...gentleman as a historical artifact."

"Then who is this?" PC wondered aloud.

"I can pull some DNA." Dupree rose.

PC pulled out her phone. "Let me check on the status of the cattle drive."

She texted Hiro Tran, the young officer who'd befriended her when the return to her hometown landed her smack in the middle of a murder investigation.

"How's the roundup?"

He texted back. "Marberger got them penned. Still fixing traffic."

She replied. "Bones at Johnson place are fresh."

"Wut"

"DuPree is here. Says bones are recent."

"K. Be there soon."

Dr. DuPree noticed the stairs going down into the earth and walked closer. "Is that a… bomb shelter?"

Justice gave a short laugh. "Yup. I call it the mushroom bunker. My Uncle Dewey built it in the 1950s, you know, when the Cold War heated up? After a while, when the nuclear winter didn't show up, everybody plum forgot about it. 'Bout five years ago, I was clearin' some brush and found the steps. Best find ever—it's perfect for growin' mushrooms."

Dupree made a little 'o' with her mouth. "Can I have a look?"

"Sure." Justice started down the stairs.

PC watched the two women disappear into the dark. Speaking of being in the dark, she should probably call her mother and give her a report.

Rose picked up before PC even heard a ring. She told her mother that Dr. DuPree was there, and Possumwood's finest were on the way. But she didn't elaborate. By the time she hung up, she could see dust rising along the gravel road. She hoped it was Tran. A few minutes later, a police cruiser and the official Tahoe of Police Chief Elwood Wilson, pulled up and stopped near PC's car.

Tran got out of the cruiser. The Chief and the Medical Examiner, Dr. McKenzie Chapman, known around town as Dr. Mack, emerged from the Tahoe.

Justice's dogs barked at the newcomers from their pen.

"…and I sell to mostly local restaurants, but there are also a few in Houston and College Station," Justice said as she led the way up the stairs.

"PPD is here." PC raised both arms above her head and waved. The three men started in her direction. When they got closer, the Chief narrowed his eyes. "Oh, look. It's Donovan. And a body. Funny how those two things seem to go hand-in-hand lately." His arm rested on his abdomen, just below his ribs.

"Good morning, Woody." PC forced a grin, then dropped it before looking at the other two men. "Dr. Mack, Tran."

What did I ever see in him all those years ago? I guess in a small-town high school, there aren't many fish, and it's more like a pond than a sea.

The men nodded back to her.

"So whatcha got? Is it an antique or a late model?" Dr. Mack asked, practically rubbing his hands together with glee before he pulled on some disposable gloves.

DuPree stepped forward. "It's definitely not an antique. Bones aren't dried out. And if you look closely, you can see artifacts where somebody tried to paint or dye the bones to make them look older."

"Interesting." Dr. Mack held up one of the arms. "Yeah. See what you mean."

To PC's left, Justice pointed down to where her composting manure piles were located, then she recounted her story of finding the skeleton to Tran and Woody.

The detective had already heard the narrative, so she wandered down to where the compost pile had been removed. She would be pleasantly surprised if she found any evidence down there, but she wouldn't know unless she looked.

Of the two remaining compost piles, one was about the size of a washing machine, the other about two-thirds its size. Both were covered in blue tarps weighted down with cinderblocks at each corner. PC rolled a block off the tarp on the largest pile and lifted the edge. A large roach scurried out of the sudden light. Pillbugs paused their perambulations. Bugs notwithstanding, the pile was nothing but a mixture of poop, dried leaves, and wood shavings. She re-secured the tarp. Then PC checked the other pile, with the same result, except that the compost was further along and less aromatic.

The area of the vacated pile had a layer of soft, dark compost, which had mostly been flattened by the bucket of the loader. The blue tarp was neatly folded and set to the side, cinderblocks on top of it.

She looked toward the house. A shed with a small tractor and a Bobcat loader inside, plus an array of tools and parts, stood between the house and the compost piles. If someone came out here during the night, Justice would probably never see them, depending, of course, on where they put their light. But how would they get to the piles? Between the camera and the dogs, they couldn't very well drive up the road and park at the locked gate without being noticed.

PC squatted and picked up a little of the compost and rolled it between her fingers. Light and crumbly, it had almost no structure. It would probably be easy to scoop some off the pile, curl the skeleton into a fetal position, then re-scoop the compost back on.

She headed back to the mushroom bunker, where Tran was taking pictures of the skeleton. He wasn't wrong for doing that, but Mr. Doe wasn't killed here, just dumped. If there was any evidence, it was much more likely to be between the compost pile and wherever the killer entered the property.

Motion caught her eye. A thin cloud of dust was moving up the dirt road. Before long, a hearse rolled through the gate. It came down the drive all the way to the tractor barn. Tran jogged over from the mushroom bunker to meet the attendants from Clay Funeral Home. PC made her way back to the skeleton, following the two men with the stretcher at a little distance. Woody and Tran stood apart from the others, talking quietly.

She stood next to Justice as the cadaver pouch was unzipped, the skeleton unfolded and zipped in. The men said nothing as they strapped it to the gurney and turned back toward their vehicle.

"Let me catch a ride back with you fellas. I want to get right on this one." Dr. Mack hurried after them.

"I told him I'd help with the post-mortem," Dr. DuPree waved as she followed the medical examiner.

"I'll go get on those reports." Tran started toward his squad. "Later, PC. Ms. Johnson."

He stopped and took some more photos of the site of the removed compost pile, the area around it, and the Bobcat before he left.

Woody typed something into his phone, then ambled up to PC and Justice. "Donovan?"

"Chief?"

"Do you have any availability to assist Officer Tran in this investigation?" Both of his hands rested on his abdomen, and he swallowed noticeably.

Justice squinted at him. "You're lookin' a little green around the gills, there, Elwood. You okay?"

"I'm fine, Miz Johnson. Thank you."

PC bit her tongue. Woody did look a bit queasy. Perhaps he wasn't used to the vibrant aromas of goats and manure compost. "Sure. Tell Tran to get in touch if he needs me."

He tipped his head toward her. "Well, if you ladies will excuse me. I have a reservation at Truffles! to take my mother to lunch. It's her birthday."

"Have fun." PC smiled.

He paused as if he were going to say something, then continued on his way.

Once he was in his Tahoe, Justice turned to PC. "C'mon in the house. I'll get us some iced tea." She started walking. "You know, your mama always said that Hilda Wilson was awful fond of you. She was so mad at her son for breakin' it off."

PC shrugged. "Lot of water under that bridge." But she had also been quite fond of Hilda. She'd wanted to go visit her, but after a certain amount of time, visiting your ex-boyfriend's mom is just weird.

Justice opened the side door, and they entered the house. PC followed her into the kitchen, where Justice retrieved a pitcher from the refrigerator and poured two glasses of tea.

She handed one to PC. "Since you're here, would you mind helping me with the ladder to the attic?"

"Of course!" PC sipped her tea.

Justice turned and made her way to the hall between the back bedroom and a bathroom. PC reached up and tugged at the cord that dangled from the ceiling. With a groan of its heavy springs, the attic's maw gaped open. PC unfolded the ladder. It seemed more rickety than average for its kind.

"You want me to go up?"

"No, no. You don't know what to look for. Just steady it a bit so I don't fall."

PC held the ladder from the back side while Justice climbed up. There was a click and a bare bulb gleamed in the darkness. Several minutes, punctuated by thumping, creaking, and metal striking metal passed.

"Eureka!" Justice came to the edge of the gap and sat, her legs resting against the rungs. "Can I hand these off to you?" She waved a large book and several smaller ones.

PC took them and set them against the wall so she could brace the ladder. Justice came down, and they folded up the stairs and closed the door.

"Look at this!" Justice picked up one of the books. "I found the family bible. But there's also some old diaries by Mamie Wharton."

"Is she related to Tom Wharton?"

"Yup. His great however many grandmother." Justice headed back to the living room and plopped on the couch.

"So, why do *you* have her things?"

"Because she was my great to the whatever aunt. Her parents were Hannah and Francois Lamartine, and her brother, Silas, was my great something grandpa. Here, have a look."

PC took the musty journal from Justice, and opened it to a random spot. The faded handwriting was both elegant and difficult to read. She started with the first entry.

October 24, 1851.

"Father, Silas, and Claude left for San Antonio early this morning. Mother, Eudora, and I had anticipated a quiet fortnight, with William here to protect us. But alas! It is not to be. Mother is frantic. William has gone missing. I fear some dreadful misadventure has befallen him. Mother and Aunt Phoebe have been talking together, urgently, but in low voices, presumably not to upset Eudora and myself. But the whispered words 'Comanche' and 'raid' have not escaped my discernment."

Chapter 5

WHAT HAPPENED TO William? Was he found, or is his disappearance what started the idea of the cursed? Does Mamie Wharton have any insight into the supposed Lamartine treasure? PC closed the old journal carefully. "Justice, do you mind if I borrow these?"

"Go right on ahead. I'll call up that McIlwraith fella and see if he still wants to have a gander at the Bible."

"So, when I was thinking about how Mr. Doe got into your compost pile, I wondered how well you know your neighbors? Do any of them strike you as weird or make you feel uncomfortable?"

"Of course not! On Friday night, I had to get goat feed and didn't get back until real late. It was good to see porch lights on as I came down the road. It gets darker than a black cat in a tar pit at midnight out here." Justice chuckled. "I'm glad you're not asking them about me—they might carry on about the crazy old goat lady." She took a sip of tea. "Well, the closest ones on this side of the road are about a mile away, to the south. That's the Gunnersons. They got more money than God, and probably, Thorne Marberger, truth be told. They have their own helipad. Don't get much use, but they have it."

PC filed that tidbit away in the back of her brain.

"To the north," Justice continued, "there's a real nice young couple. Mr. Turner sells organic herbs and greens to the fancy grocery stores. His missus is an artist, makes gorgeous stained-glass and pottery. Look at the kitchen window—that's one of her pieces."

PC stood up and walked over to look. Blotches of colored light stained the white countertop where the sun shone through a glass ruby-throated hummingbird visiting a red Turk's cap flower. "Did she have a booth at Maifest?" PC remembered the beautiful designs she'd seen at the festival yesterday afternoon.

"Probably. She sells stuff on the computer, but she does all the fests and fairs. Yup. Real nice folks." Justice nodded. "Now my cousin, Melvin Stewart, is across the street. His oldest daughter and her husband moved in with him when his wife, Cora Lee, died." Justice shook her head. "That girl's husband, I don't think he's ever done a lick of work in his life. And my neighbor to the back, Ben Masters, he keeps to himself. Always been nice enough to me. I give him a ride into town ever now and again. He's helped me out once or twice around the farm."

PC returned to her seat. "What does he do? Is he a farmer?"

"Don't rightly know. Mostly trees between my back fence and his house. His plot used to be ours, but my granddad sold off that twenty acres a while back. Me and my cousins used to play in that cabin when we was kids. There's also an abandoned farmhouse— you can't see it from here—but we was sure that thing was haunted, never set foot in there. Anyway, I believe Ben mentioned one time he's got solar panels, though. Oh, and he was in the military. Don't recall which branch."

PC took a sip of tea, but the ice slammed into her mouth, causing her to jump and spill the last bit of her drink onto her shirt. She stood up, making sure she hadn't spilled anything on the couch.

"Lemme grab you a paper towel."

Justice got up and hot-footed it into the kitchen. When she returned, she handed PC a whole roll of towels.

"You should get me a sippy cup next time." PC blotted her shirt. *At least I didn't get any on the journals.*

Justice gave a soft laugh. Then she chewed her lip. "Do you think they'll be able to use dental records to identify that fella?"

PC handed the paper towel roll back to her. "The problem is that there's no dental record database. You have to have an idea of who the decedent is so you can go to their dentist and get their records to compare with the teeth. They should have no trouble getting DNA, but if he's not in CODIS..." PC shrugged.

"Codas? Isn't that somethin' in music? Seems like a hundred years since I took piano."

"C-O-D-I-S is the FBI's Combined DNA Index System. There's also a few private DNA databases, but there's no guarantee he'll be in those, either." PC squeezed the damp paper towels in her hand. "I appreciate the tea, and the journals." She picked up the old diaries. "I'll get them back to you soon. But as I'm supposed to be helping Officer Tran, I really should get down to the station. I'm going to run by Mama's house to drop these off and change my shirt first, though."

PC sat in the conference room at Possumwood PD, using a laptop to search through missing persons reports. The preliminary autopsy report sat on the table next to the computer. Dr. DuPree had noted that she thought Mr. Doe stood about 5'8" when he was alive. A few arthritic changes in the joints made her think he was older, but not elderly. Maybe fifties or sixties.

In the last forty-eight hours, within a one-hundred-mile radius, four people had been reported missing: 1) A sixteen year old girl, who had been found safe at her boyfriend's house; 2) A ninety-two year old woman, who'd started wandering due to dementia and was located by K9s; 3) A five-year old boy whose aunt forgot to pick him up at daycare; and 4) a fifty year old man who'd gone camping at Lake Sommerville. Turned out he'd dropped his phone into the lake while reeling in a catfish, then had car trouble on the way home.

She widened the search. No one that matched the bones turned up. PC didn't hold out much hope that John Doe's DNA would get a CODIS hit. Perhaps they'd luck out with one of the genealogy databases. It wasn't like she could pass out *Have You Seen Me?* fliers with a picture of his skull and expect to get a reasonable response. Unless…

PC made a call to the Texas Rangers at Department of Public Safety headquarters in Austin. Most people think drivers' licenses and highway patrol when they think of the DPS, but they have forensics labs and investigative teams that help small jurisdictions with criminal investigations.

Eventually, she got put through to the Forensic Art group.

"Yes, ma'am. My name is Detective Sergeant PC Donovan. I'm working with the Possumwood PD, and we have an unidentified decedent, just skeletal remains. I was hoping we could get a facial reconstruction."

"Please hold."

After what felt like several hours, the woman came back on the line. "Yes ma'am. The artists are actually testing some new software specifically for UID reconstruction. We can send a tech out tomorrow to do a scan. Not sure how long the render will take—there's a couple of jobs in front of you."

"Perfect."

PC gave the woman her cell number and the address of Possumwood PD before hanging up. She was at the end of what she could do with the information she had, so she sent an email to Tran and Woody, apprising them about the facial reconstruction.

While the scene was still fresh in her mind, she decided to make a sketch of where the skeleton was found at Justice's.

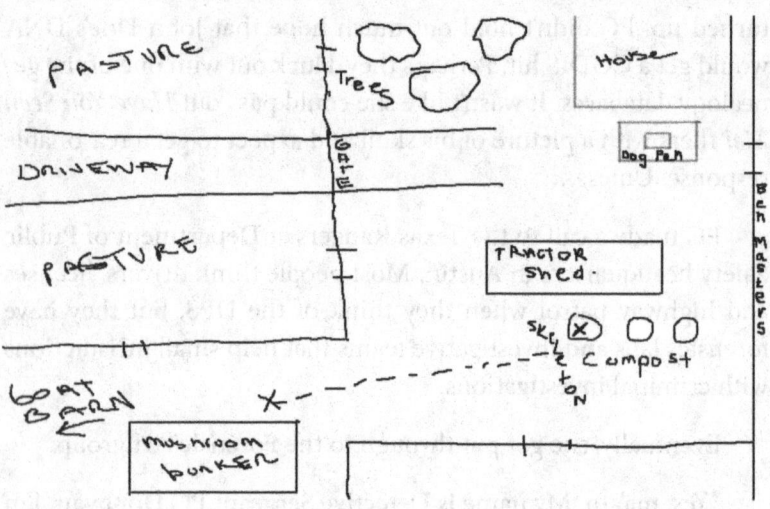

Her mind shifted back to the journals Justice had loaned her. A trip to the Quenton Plantation Historical Park might fill in some details. She used the twenty-minute drive to think about the supposed Lamartine treasure. Three weeks ago, an old skeleton from around the Civil War had been discovered at Mayor Phineas Scott's house, in an abandoned well. It wasn't easily identifiable, but it could be Francois de Lamartine, a diplomat who'd fled France after a scandalous love affair and somehow ended up in Possumwood. He'd built himself a very fine house, not a chateau, but certainly a mansion.

Lamartine had come to town with a great deal of money, then started his own freight business before settling down with the empresario's oldest daughter. The town's father was delighted to have such a well-to-do son-in-law and seemed to grow richer himself. Rumor had it that Lamartine had hidden away a secret treasure that he'd brought from France. Some said it was a gift, others said it was stolen. When Lamartine vanished without a trace in 1860, people mostly fell into two camps, those who believed he abandoned his family to escape the coming Civil War, and the others who were sure it was foul play. A few, however, blamed it on his cursed treasure, saying the Devil had most likely come to collect his due.

Lamartine had also made a set of six paintings. Two were at the Quenton Plantation. The Biersal Brew Pub, Ada Dotson, and Phineas Scott had one painting each. The location of the last one remained a mystery. All of the known paintings had one thing in common: in the background, there was a woman dressed in blue, doing something incongruous with the rest of the painting. PC was sure the Blue Lady was a clue, but she didn't have the decoder ring to figure it out. Would the missing picture hold the key?

Then it occurred to PC that the forensic artist tech could also scan the skull they found in the well. She supposed that a facial reconstruction for the well skeleton hadn't occurred to her because anyone who had known Lamartine had been dead for over a hundred years. That flier wouldn't generate any leads, either. But there were portraits of him. Perhaps she'd call Dr. DuPree and ask if they'd already set this up, since she and Dr. McIlwraith had taken those remains back to Austin with them.

She pulled into the parking space and shut off the car. The short walk up to the ticket window was pleasantly warm, although an occasional northerly gust gave her goose flesh as it blew its cool breath on her skin.

She bought her ticket and made her way up the steps to the grand entry of the plantation house. Inside, the place smelled authentically aged. Not musty, just… old. It was an aroma common to all historic sites. She leaned against the wall and studied the brochure and its map. There wasn't a dedicated Possumwood Museum, so the Quenton Plantation held not just its own artifacts, but those from a number of historical periods and prominent figures from the town.

PC looked at the twin curved staircases sweeping up to the second floor. A corridor with a red floral carpet gaped in the back wall, between the stairs. To her right was the grand ballroom. The kitchen wing lay to her left.

Might as well start at the beginning of the self-guided tour.

The ballroom was first. Large paintings, mostly of the prominent families of the early nineteenth century, dominated the walls. A few landscapes and still lifes filled in any gaps. The floor was mostly kept clear, so the intricate parquet inlays could be admired. Each square used three different kinds of wood to create a dramatic pattern. A handful of free-standing display cases showed off jewelry, shoes, and hair accessories partygoers might have worn. Six mannequins stood in one corner, four ladies and two gentlemen frozen in conversation, resplendent in their ballgowns and suits, the height of nineteenth-century fashion.

PC cringed as her tennies squeaked on the highly polished dance floor. Time to get to the next room. She exited the ballroom and found herself in a corridor. On the left side, a heavy oak door led to a billiards room. On the right was a drawing room. She flitted from exhibit to exhibit, taking in the artifacts, but keeping her eye out for the Lamartines.

At last, she found them. In the upstairs parlor. One was the *Battle of Mirabella Creek* that Wilma Gatewood had used in her acrylic painting lessons last month. PC studied the original. Horse soldiers charged. Settlers raised muskets. Smoke blurred the scene. And there she was, the Blue Lady, serenely emptying a pail of ashes into a big tub. A red cardinal perched in a nearby tree and watched her.

Was there an order to the paintings? Which one was first?

On the adjacent wall, the other Lamartine, creatively named *Courthouse,* showed a detailed portrait of the Mirabella County courthouse, in all its European-style glory. In the background, the Lady in Blue lowered a teapot into a well, observed by a cardinal. Is that the well from Phineas Scott's house, or is it just a generic well? Was there ever a well like that on the courthouse property? There wasn't one now.

A pair of Lamartine's dueling pistols was displayed in the corner. PC examined them. Two flintlock handguns with polished wood grips nestled into a green felt-lined case. There were some accompanying pieces that PC had no idea what they might be used for, but she recognized the bullet mold.

"Oh!"

PC turned around to see the curator standing in the doorway. "Afternoon, Dinah Mae."

She looked like a cornered rat. "Detective Donovan. I didn't expect to see you here."

"I'm just trying to refresh my memory on the history of Possumwood." She looked at the pistols. "What about these? Was Lamartine ever in a duel?"

"Oh. Those are fairly new, only had them a couple of years. That should be on the display plaque. But that's really all I know. It was nice talking to you, but I really have to get goin'."

"Bye," PC said to Dinah Mae's quickly retreating form.

Eventually, she made it back to the first floor, and of course, exited through the gift shop. PC searched the poster prints, hoping there would be prints of at least some of the other Lamartines. But no luck. The only ones they had were of the two in the museum, and Rose already had prints of those. PC was eager to get home and read Mamie's journal.

Menagerie managed, family fed, and body bathed, PC settled down with the journal she'd picked up the day before. The faded handwriting was in a spidery cursive, with flourishes on some of the capital letters. It was slow going, so PC decided she'd try to only read one or two entries at a go.

October 25, 1851

William is still missing. Mother is frantic. Uncle Mux has requested the aid of the Texas Rangers, in the event that our poor William has been kidnapped by the Comanche. There has been no rumor of them in months, not since they passed to the north after their last incursion into Mexico. My younger brother has always let his curiosity get the better of him, and I fear it has cost him dearly this time. Since my uncle has become the mayor of Possumwood, my dear aunt Phoebe has become preoccupied with the threat of Indian raids. She married a Marberger! He is a strong man, and she should not fear so. I have every faith that the Rangers shall keep us from calamity. However, while they are afield, I shall keep my own counsel and pursue my own exploration. William cannot be far—he has no horse or conveyance. But where shall I begin my search?

Chapter 6

WHAT HAPPENED TO *William?* PC was curious, but her eyelids drooped. She copied the entries she'd already read to a piece of paper, yawning the whole time. When she arrived at the station in the morning, she'd type them up. That'd make it easier when she read them again later.

After her morning chores were done, she showered and headed downtown to the cop shop. Annie, the dispatcher, buzzed her in and PC got to work at her borrowed laptop. She found her own sleepy handwriting was nearly as hard to read as Mamie's. She was getting her second cup of coffee in the break room when her text chime sounded.

"Det. Donovan—this is Adam Eastwood DPS Forensic Art. ETA 30 min."

"10-4. Meet at Clay's Funeral Home."

PC texted Dr. Mack to tell him the tech was arriving soon. She finished her coffee and hoofed it over to the mortuary. Dr. Mack was waiting for her in the lobby.

"Mornin', detective." His eyes twinkled above his broad smile.

"Good morning, Dr. Mack. Have you been able to find out any more about our John Doe?"

"No, nothing Dr. DuPree had not already noted. Collected some DNA. We may luck out and get a CODIS hit, but otherwise, there's not much we can do until we have some idea of who to compare it to. Good idea you had, about the facial reconstruction."

"Thanks. We've had good luck with it in Houston. <u>DPS</u> said they were testing some facial reconstruction software, so hopefully that'll speed things up." PC gave a little half shrug.

"I've heard of that. Some of it's pretty good."

The door opened, and a young man entered, wearing a dark suit. "Am I early?"

Dr. Mack gestured for the man to follow. "No, you're right on time." He started toward one corridor.

PC gave him a quick scan. "Don't you have some equipment to bring in?"

The man frowned. "Equipment?"

Dr. Mack turned around. "Are you Adam?"

He shook his head. "No. I'm Tyus."

Dr. Mack's eyes widened. "So sorry. There's a visitation down that hall." He pointed down a corridor. "That's probably what you're looking for."

The young man nodded and trudged in that direction.

Dr. Mack rubbed his forehead. "I'm glad you said something. If I'd taken him into the embalming room…"

The door opened again, and another young man entered, this time dressed in a khaki polo with a DPS logo and pulling a rolling bag behind him. "I'm looking for a Detective Donovan?"

"You Adam?"

"Yes."

"I'm Detective Donovan, and this is Dr. Mack, the Medical Examiner."

They all shook hands, and Dr. Mack led the way to the embalming room.

While Adam was setting up his equipment, Dr. Mack retrieved Mr. Doe and laid the body bag on the table. The technician arranged the skeleton and got to work with his 3D scanner. It looked a lot like an oversized heavy-duty stapler, and it didn't take him long to do the job.

Adam looked at the screen on his laptop. "I think I got a good scan. Do you know if there's wi-fi? I'd like to get this uploaded to the server so the software can be doing the pre-processing while I'm traveling back to the office."

"I think there is. Let me ask." Dr. Mack pulled out his phone and sent a text.

Moments later, a solemn Redd Clay, dressed in his black funeral director suit, came into the embalming room. "Yes, Doctor? You were inquiring about wi-fi?"

"Mr. Eastwood needs to upload some images to his server in Austin, if that's okay with you?"

"Of course. Of course. If you scan for networks, you should find one called ClayGuest."

Adam dragged his finger on the touchpad. "There it is."

"The password is Angels. That's with a capital A."

"Thank you very much."

"Now, if you have nothing else, I must get back to the visitation."

Adam tapped keys.

Dr. Mack responded to a text message.

PC looked awkwardly around the embalming room. Mirabella County Hospital had closed years ago. Clay's Funeral Home had most of the equipment a morgue would require, but the county did have to spring for a hanging scale. There weren't a lot of suspicious deaths in Mirabella County. Or the surrounding three. Dr. Mack was a retired pathologist and did medical exam work for the four-county district on a contract basis, out of his makeshift morgue here in the funeral home. If a case was especially dicey, he sent it to the Harris County Forensics Institute in Houston or the Department of Public Safety forensics lab. This one may be heading to one of those.

The doctor slipped the phone back into his pocket. "My wife and her never-ending grocery list."

PC smiled politely. "Do you have any guesses as to when our Doe might have died?"

"Without markers like body temp, rigor, and lividity, it's pretty hard to tell. But there's a lot of moisture in his bones—I would be surprised if it was more than two or three days."

"So somewhere between Thursday and Sunday morning?"

"I think so. But once the flesh was removed, and that takes some time, the bones would have to dry enough to apply the colorant, then that would take some time to dry. I would expect those operations took up all of Saturday, at the very least."

Adam closed his laptop. "Alrighty, my files are uploaded, so I'm going to hit the road. We'll email you a PNG when the render's done."

"Thanks. You wouldn't happen to know if there's been any requests to scan the other skeleton we found here a couple of weeks ago? Dr. DuPree—"

"You mean Wellboy? Yeah. I did him last week. Because he's Civil War era, we 3D printed the skull, and Louis is working on an actual physical reconstruction."

"That seems like a lot of extra effort."

Adam shrugged. "You can put him in a museum."

Dr. Mack cleared his throat. "I'm off to Marberger's to do the bidding of my lovely bride. Nice meeting you, Adam. Looking forward to seeing that render."

PC and Adam followed Dr. Mack down the corridor and out to the parking lot. She waved to them both as they got into their respective cars. The funeral home was only a few blocks from the police station, so she'd walked. She was about halfway back when Tran's cruiser pulled up alongside her.

"Hey PC! You want to run a call with me?"

That depends. She raised a hand to shade her eyes from the bright sun. "What is it?"

"Treasure hunters."

Not something you see every day. She opened the door and slid inside.

"Treasure hunters? Really?"

"Yep. Apparently, after the skeleton was found in the well, one of the local kids made a video about the Lamartine treasure and put it up on social media. Now we have yahoos with metal detectors running around."

"Where are they?"

"Thorne Marberger's place."

PC cringed. Vindictive was his middle name. Thorne would persecute them to the fullest extent of the law.

Tran slowed to take a corner. "Dispatch said he's got them locked in the tack room of his horse barn."

PC could picture him putting a bar through the door handles and keeping the terrified treasure hunters from leaving. "I don't envy them."

"Do you know the Marbergers?"

"Thorne's brother, Cortland, married my mother's sister, Lily, so we're not exactly related, but he is my uncle's brother, so… that being said, Uncle Cort and Aunt Lily moved to Vermont shortly after they tied the knot, and I didn't see much of them growing up. The Marbergers weren't so keen on Cort marrying a commoner, but they eventually got over it. Thorne's wife, Sylvia, does look in on Mama from time to time. But we don't do Thanksgiving or anything like that."

"That's the thing I had trouble with when I moved here. Half the people are related in some way or another."

"Thanks for coming to expand the gene pool. The City of Possumwood appreciates your service."

Tran blushed.

Okay, that was probably a step too far. "So how are the wedding plans going?"

"You'll have to ask Annie. As far as I know, everything's good. Still trying to nail down a date at the Afters. They're crazy busy Halloween through Christmas."

PC's head bobbed as the car rumbled over a rough spot. "Well, if you were having a Halloween wedding, the Afters would be the place to have it."

"They do have the haunted weekend around Halloween, but they go 110% for Christmas. Looks like a Christmas decoration warehouse exploded all over it."

When PC had left town for college, the old Victorian was a rotting hulk. She was glad that Simone and Caitlyn Reynolds had lovingly salvaged the old place. It looked like it was straight out of a Southern Living Magazine photoshoot now.

Tran turned off the road onto a grand paved driveway. About fifty feet in, an elaborate fieldstone gateway, complete with twin waterfalls, one on each side of the pavement, was pure Marberger in its extravagance. The officer rolled the window down and pressed a button on the security panel.

A male voice crackled out of the speaker. "Can I help you?"

"Possumwood PD. We're here about your intruders."

The gate swung open. Tran slipped the car into drive and continued down the blacktop. White four-rail fences ran alongside the drive, and shaggy pecan trees guarded the pastures, making big pools of shade for Thorne's livestock. Black cows lounged under the Spanish moss-draped boughs, chewing their cuds.

The main house stood on a gentle hill. It was a boxy, post-modern structure, with lots of bamboo, cedar, and glass. As the hill sloped away, PC could see the horse barn a hundred yards or so away. Tran saw it too, because he continued down the drive in that direction. He pulled up next to a black dually truck and cut the engine.

Thorne Marberger strolled out of the barn with a shotgun on his shoulder. "It's about time you got here." He looked at PC and cocked his head, like a dog trying to hone in on a distant sound. "Primrose? What are you doing here?"

"I'm doing some consulting work while I'm in town."

"I see. Sylvia said your mother had broken her hip. How is Rose?"

"She's doing good. Feisty as ever. So, what about these treasure hunters?"

"Well, Jimmy called me, said there were three males that had entered the perimeter fence. Two of them appeared to be carrying metal detectors. They didn't realize they were getting in the pasture with JoJo." Thorne chuckled.

"Who is JoJo?" Tran asked.

"He is two thousand pounds of Brangus bull. And he does not like strangers. Anyway, by the time I got down there in the quad, they were running through the field like scalded haints, with JoJo hot on their heels. Dropped all their stuff as they ran. I'll have to go pick it up. Can you cite them for littering?"

"I don't know about that." Tran's head tilted to one side.

Thorne started back toward the barn. "They were here yesterday, too. Back side of the property. They were the ones who left a gate open and let the cows out."

"Oh." Tran looked at PC as Thorne turned to open the barn doors.

She shrugged.

The inside of the barn was nicer than a lot of houses. The center aisle was concrete and recently swept. All the interior structure was polished oak, with black metal fittings and latches. The wood stopped at about four feet in height, then the inner walls were topped with bars so the horses could see their fellow stablemates. No convenience was neglected for Thorne's equines and their caretakers.

PC's eyes followed the stairway up.

"We have a lounge up there," Thorne said. "Kitchenette, restrooms, showers, TV area, pool table. There's also a control room, for monitoring the cameras."

"Oh, you have security cameras for the barn?" Tran looked at the rafters.

"We usually only use them when we have mares about to foal." Thorne stopped at a sliding door. "They're in here."

Tran knocked on the door. "Possumwood Police. I'm going to open the door. Stand back."

He undid the snap that was fitted into the padlock slot and slowly slid the door open. Three young men, sweaty and bedraggled, sat on the floor. PC estimated they were in their late teens, early twenties. One was covered in grass, as if he'd taken a tumble. She was mostly successful in keeping her laughter in check.

"You go with her." Tran pointed to the grassy boy. "You come with me." He pointed to another of the group. "We'll be with *you* in a few minutes," he told the last one.

PC led her subject to the far end of the barn. Tran took his out toward his squad. They'd had plenty of time to collaborate on their story, but if they had spun a web of fiction, it was unlikely to hold. *Two can keep a secret, if one of them is dead. Don't even try three.*

She pulled out the Moleskine notebook she always carried in her bag. Force of habit after twenty-five years in Homicide.

"You seem to have gotten yourself in a bit of a pickle. I'm Detective Donovan. Let's see if we can get it straightened out, huh? What's your name?"

He stared at his shoes. "Morgan Clovis, ma'am."

"Do you have any ID?"

He pulled a thin wallet out of his back pocket and fumbled for his driver's license. His hand shook as he handed it over.

PC studied the picture, then studied his face. They matched. Then she noticed the address. "You're from Horice? Are you related to the gentleman with the car dealership?"

Morgan seemed to shrink into himself. "That's my dad."

PC handed the license back. "Would you like to tell me how you came to be playing bull rush in Mr. Marberger's field this morning?"

Morgan sighed. "My dad bought the metal detectors for when we go to the beach, go camping, stuff like that. Usually, it's just normal loose change, but one time, we got a diamond ring, and another time there was an old coin, from like the 1800s."

"What were you looking for this morning?"

"It was on YouTube. There's supposed to be some hidden treasure around here."

"Do you believe everything you see on YouTube?"

Morgan shook his head. "No, ma'am."

"You have to get permission to come on someone's property. You're old enough to know that. Were you here yesterday?"

"Yes."

PC kept her questions conversational. "Okay. Where were you?"

"Back side of this property. We didn't mean to let the cows out. It was a total accident."

"I understand. You guys are in a lot of trouble, though. First of all, you're not allowed to take something that's more than a hundred years old—it's considered an archaeological artifact. Second, you're on private property, so whatever you find belongs to the owner. And last, you trespassed onto someone else's property with the intent of taking something that didn't belong to you, so that bumps it up to burglary."

Morgan swallowed hard. "Wh-what's going to happen to us?"

"That depends on whether Mr. Marberger wants to press charges." *And Thorne will delight in pressing charges.*

PC glanced down the aisleway and saw the kid that Tran had been questioning sitting on a big tack trunk in front of one of the stalls. The officer was now speaking with the last boy.

"Alright. Why don't you go sit by your friend?"

Morgan nodded and hurried to his partner in crime. Once all three were sitting on the box, under the baleful surveillance of Thorne Marberger, PC, and Tran moved out of earshot.

PC ran a hand through her hair. "What's the plan?"

"Marberger wants to charge them with everything he possibly can. We're going to have to take them to the station and call their parents, and let the parents deal with attorneys. If it was up to me, I'd just cite them for trespassing and let everybody get on with their day."

So, two in the back of the squad and one in the front? That didn't leave any room for her. "I guess Thorne will be coming into town. Let me see if I can bum a ride with him."

Tran nodded.

PC strode down the aisle. "Thorne?" she asked as soon as she got near. "Are you headed straight into town with Officer Tran?"

"Of course."

"Can I catch a ride with you?"

44

"I don't see why not. We can follow him in case they try anything."

"Sure." These were three terrified boys. The only thing they were going to try was not to pee themselves with fear. "I'll help him get them situated in the car."

There didn't seem to be a reason to cuff them, so Tran didn't. They buckled themselves in, and the officer started the car.

"Let's go, Primrose." Thorne slapped his thigh, as if he were encouraging a dog to come.

He got into the black truck, so PC did the same. Then he stopped at the house and started to climb out.

"I thought we were going to the station?"

He gave her an incredulous look. "We are. But I can't take the *farm* truck into town."

Thorne slammed his door, so PC got out and trotted around the front of the truck. He was getting into a blue BMW, so PC hurried over, so she didn't get left behind. The engine purred to life and Thorne quickly caught up with Tran's cruiser.

PC watched the four-board fence go by. "Do you really think Lamartine's treasure is hidden here?"

"Here on my farm, or here in Possumwood?"

"Either."

Thorne harrumphed. "Lamartine. He was a con man from the get-go. My Great-Great-Great-Great-Great-Grandmother Phoebe's sister was married to him. Aunt Hannah. Obviously, I never met her. But she was very well regarded. Lamartine, not so much. Phoebe's husband, Mux Marberger, was the one who started that freight business. When he was appointed mayor, he asked his brother-in-law, Lamartine, to run it for him, but once he got his hands on it, he never gave it back. Lamartine's treasure may very well be Marberger's treasure."

"Huh." *That was added incentive for Thorne to keep treasure hunters off his land.*

"Yeah. You don't much hear that story. It's all Lamartine this, Lamartine that. It's *so romantic*—" he swirled his head around and used a falsetto voice "—but he ran away from his English girlfriend and hid out in Texas. He didn't waste much time in getting married, once he got here, either."

Families being families, there was always going to be some bad blood somewhere. "It's a shame we don't have a time machine."

Thorne snorted.

Except...I kind of do. I have Mamie's journals.

After she typed the report for her interview with the Clovis boy, there wasn't much else for PC to do at the station, so she decamped to Rose's house to read another entry from the musty diary. Mamie might just have a clue about her father's alleged treasure.

October 26, 1851

A most extraordinary thing has happened this morning. The clerk's wife had packed him a hearty luncheon in a wicker basket. He left his station for a few moments to retrieve a document, and when he returned, the basket had vanished. He was so astonished that he ran from the room to fetch the judge. When the twain entered the clerk's office, the basket had returned, but not the lunch! While the judge was assisting the clerk, an apple he'd picked from his very own tree disappeared from his chambers. Not a soul had been seen entering or leaving the building. Someone said it must surely be a kobold, which has been explained to me as being a goblin of German extraction.

Chapter 7

MONDAY AFTERNOON, TUESDAY, and Wednesday slogged by with no news about either Wellboy, as the DPS tech had called him, or John Doe. The only highlight had been Wednesday night darts with Drew. Thursday had finally lumbered into frame, bringing with it an early alarm and an hour-long drive into Houston. PC and Rose sat in the waiting room of Rose's orthopedist, so Dr. Thompson could check the progress of the last procedure on her hip.

PC had tried texting Dr. McIlwraith, to find out if the Wellboy reconstruction was completed. She was eager to see if it really looked like Francois Lamartine. So far, no reply, but cell service in the Big Bend area was spotty at best. And he could be taking the opportunity to unplug and unwind.

She was about to try Dr. DuPree when the nurse called them back.

PC had to push the wheelchair a little faster than she liked, just to keep up. Rose had already been X-rayed, and now the nurse took her blood pressure and temperature.

Dr. Thompson breezed into the room. "Good morning, Rose!" He nodded to PC, then turned back to his patient. "How is your hip feeling?"

"Better. It's better. Although I do still have a little trouble getting around. My balance seems to be off."

The orthopedist nodded. "Let's have a look at your films."

He turned on a computer, and the X-rays were projected to a screen on the wall. Dr. Thompson studied the images, nodding his head and typing a few notes into the file.

"Rose, your implant looks very good. I'm pleased with it. The problem doesn't appear to be caused by anything around the surgical site. Could I get you to stand up and take a few steps?"

PC locked the wheelchair while Rose stood up, then hobbled to the exam table and back.

The doctor scowled. "Let's take your shoes off. And stay seated."

Rose did as she was told. The doctor sat on his wheelie stool and glided over to her. He took her ankles and gently straightened her legs. There was some clucking and scowling.

"Rose. I think I see what the problem is. Your right leg is about half an inch longer than your left. I'm sorry. Sometimes it happens with this surgery. We'll get you a custom lift for your shoe, then I'd like to see you back in thirty days to see how you're coping with it."

Rose sighed and nodded.

"The tech will come in and take your measurements in a minute. You take care, and I'll see you in June."

Not really the ideal diagnosis, but at least she didn't have to have another procedure.

PC pulled into a parking space at Cordite's vet. "Do you want to wait in the car, or come inside? I'll leave the AC on if you want to stay here."

"It'll probably take less time for you to go in and get the pills than it will take me to get out of the car."

"Mama, you know that's not true. But if you prefer to wait, that's fine." PC left the car running but locked the door. The receptionist's desk should still be in range for the key fob, so the engine would stay on.

She looked over her shoulder as she got out of the SUV. The last thing she needed was for Rose to get depressed about her progress.

An electronic chime sounded as she opened the door.

"How may I help you?" The receptionist, whose neon red hair tumbled out of sight down her back, smiled.

"PC Donovan. I called earlier to get some heartworm pills for Cordite."

"Yes, ma'am. I have them right here. Will that be cash or credit?"

PC slid her debit card into the little machine.

The device took an abnormally long time to process her payment. While she waited, her eyes scanned the waiting area. A bright blue poster caught her eye. A bone-shaped dog treat wore a flowing red cape. Text above it read, "Master your dog's stinky breath with FreshBonz."

The machine chimed at her, telling PC to remove her card.

The receptionist handed her the receipt and box of medication. "Have a great afternoon."

Cordite didn't particularly like his monthly heartworm treatment, but he could not resist a cream cheese treat. Another errand she had to run. Get the dog a box of cream cheese. May as well get bagels while she was at the store.

She tossed her bag and the prescription on the back seat of the car. "All done. Let's get you home."

"Can we stop by Brandee's for some fudge?"

"Of course, Mama." PC inwardly cringed. Last time, she'd struggled to talk her mother out of a mirror-mosaic-encrusted-cow skull clock. Yesiree, a body could get everything they needed (and a lot of things they didn't) for a road trip at the travel plaza paradise.

But it was tough to beat their bathrooms.

PC took a long cut and drove by her own house. It was disconcerting to see the small blue Honda in the driveway. It was still weird to be a landlord. She'd expected to be in Possumwood for three months, four at the outside, while her mother recovered from her hip replacement. She hadn't expected to still be there in May, and certainly not until June, but here she was. Or wasn't, as the case may be. Technically, Felicity, the grad student, was just renting a room, but with PC out of town, she had the whole house to herself.

There were no beer bottles or other party debris in the front yard, as one might fear with a college student, and the place looked fine. Felicity had been collecting PC's mail and sending it all to her once a week, so the detective didn't have to come into town and fetch it. She was still deciding if that was good or bad. What was it she was feeling? Homesickness? Nostalgia? PC sighed as she exited the neighborhood and pulled onto Heights Boulevard.

They made it home with only two boxes of fudge, a pair of bluebonnet dish towels, and a large bag of chocolate covered popcorn. Once Rose was settled in, PC grabbed the grocery list that was stuck on the refrigerator door with a magnet. She hastily scribbled "cream cheese" at the end.

"Alright, Mama. I'm going to Marberger's. Is there anything you need, other than what's on the list?"

"No, I don't think so."

PC took Cordite out for a potty break before she headed to the grocery store. Phineas Scott's house wasn't exactly on the way, but she was hoping she might find Dr. McIlwraith's assistant, Cooper Downing, there. He'd been helping out with the archaeological dig. Perhaps he'd have some information about the reconstruction on the well skeleton.

She rang Scott's doorbell. No one came to the door. PC glanced at her FlitBit. It was 2:30. The mayor was obviously still at work. She walked around the side of the house to the chain-link fence to see if Downing was in the back yard working. He was not.

PC noted that the wooden cover of the old well had been re-placed, sans chain, and the concrete planter had been righted and re-filled with flowers, although it was on the ground now, instead of sitting on top of the well cover.

He's probably on vacation because his boss is on vacation. Makes sense, I guess.

She tried McIlwraith's number again. Straight to voice mail. An uneasy feeling crept over her, and she tried to brush it off. *Just because* you *don't know where he is doesn't mean he's missing.* Still, there was a fresh skeleton and a number of people who'd left town right before it turned up: Rocky's homeless friend—Kyle Lennon, Dr. McIlwraith, and Cooper Downing. They were all males.

But what about motive, means, and opportunity? She didn't have enough information to draw any conclusions about that. Perhaps it would be helpful to spend some time looking into the backgrounds of those three. It would probably be a dead end, but it was a task for tomorrow, anyway.

Once evening chores and dinner were finished, she transcribed the next entry from Mamie's journal.

October 27, 1851

Mother had gone to fetch some butter from Aunt Phoebe's house. I was outside, securing the livestock, when Eudora came running at her fastest gait, and screaming to boot. I tried to calm my sister down so as to inquire about the trouble. I was unable to comprehend her gibberings, so I followed her into the house, where she crept into the drawing room. She pointed to the fireplace. A fire had been laid and was providing a most gladsome glow to the room. Nothing seemed to be amiss. I gave her a questioning look, but she raised her index finger to her lips. I waited for some short time, and then there was a loud rap from the chimney! The noise did not sound to my ear as an animal scrambling in the brickwork. For good measure, I approached the wall behind the fireplace and knocked in reply. The fireplace responded with another loud rap! I was so astonished that I nearly came to grief over the brass firewood rack. I shouted, "Who are you?" but received no response. Had the Kobold paid us a visit? Or, and I hardly dare to think it, was it the sad ghost of William, come to bid us farewell? It was then that Mother returned, and the knocking ceased.

Chapter 8

PC's TEXT CHIME jangled. She sat in the conference room of the Possumwood PD, staring at the ME's report on the skeletonized remains found at Justice's farm. There had to be some clues there, but she wasn't seeing them. The bones had been treated with a common, easily obtainable leather dye, presumably to make them look antique and slow down the investigation. Why hurry if, like Wellboy, their owner had been dead for a hundred years or more?

She looked at her phone. Her mother was asking if she wouldn't mind swinging by Lucky Wok for take-out on her way home.

PC replied. "Sure. What do you want?"

Rose answered. "Pineapple fried rice for me, Singapore noodles for Terry. Egg roll. Wonton soup."

She told Annie she was taking a lunch break as she left.

Lucky Wok didn't have an online ordering feature, but PC called ahead when she got to her car. She added a lunch special for herself to Rose's order. The food was not quite ready when she arrived, so she spent a few minutes studying the immense aquarium, populated with orange and white goldfish, that separated the cashier from the dining area. A serene Buddha meditated at one end of the tank. A Chinese dragon reared its maned head at the other, pearl clutched in its claws and bubbles escaping its mouth.

"Ah! Primrose. Your order is ready." A middle-aged Asian woman held out a large plastic bag.

PC recognized her mother's next-door neighbor instantly. "Hi, Lin. How's the painting going?"

Lin grinned. "I'm working on an oil for the Settler's Day show next month."

PC took the bag. It was heavier than she'd anticipated, and she moved her free hand to support the bottom. "Looking forward to seeing it. Thanks!"

"I put some sesame balls in there specially for Rose."

"Thank you. She loves everything you cook."

PC turned to go, then hesitated. "Lin, when you buy meat, do you get whole carcasses, or is it already processed?"

Lin's brow wrinkled. "We do both. Why do you ask?"

"Case I'm working on. Just trying to get an idea of how long it takes to butcher… an animal, like… maybe a pig."

"If you know what you're doing, three, four hours."

"That helps a lot. Thanks." She gave an exaggerated nod as she left.

PC had only dealt with one dismemberment case in all her years in Homicide, and time of death wasn't an issue then. This John Doe could have been killed as late as Saturday morning. The bones would have to dry for hours, possibly a whole day, so the dye would stick. Then the dye would have to cure before the bones were moved Saturday night. How long would that take? An hour? A day? She looked up and realized she had passed Rose's house three blocks ago. Grumbling to herself, she turned on the next street. Two wrongs don't make a right, but three lefts do.

She pulled into the driveway and took a moment to clear her head before she served lunch. Cordite gave a few yips as she opened the screen door. He probably needed a potty break—he danced around her feet and nearly tripped her up.

"Okay, okay. Give me a minute."

Rose and Terry were sitting on the couch together, holding hands. PC set the food down on the coffee table.

"Hey, Terry."

"Hey." He released Rose's hand and sat up on the edge of the sofa.

PC gave him a brief smile. "Would you mind getting any silverware or plates you need? I'm going to take Cordie out for a pit stop right quick."

"Sure. No problem."

The little dog trotted ahead of PC to the back door. When she opened it, he scanned for Rose's four semi-feral cats before he scooted through. The coast was clear. He whirled around in a circle across the threshold, then dashed across the back porch and leaped off the middle of the three steps into the grass.

PC glanced around at the menagerie. Pavarotti, the rooster, and his best gal Clementine, a plump orange hen, were scratching around in the flowerbed where Rose's azaleas had returned to their standard nondescript shrub state after their explosion of pale pink earlier in the spring. Arthur and Guinevere snoozed under the overhang of the shed. Hazel basked in the sun on a bed of dark green clover.

Cordite accomplished his mission and was now sniffing around the yard. PC debated about leaving him to roam while she had her lunch, but Rose's fence wasn't exactly dog proof. The detective could bring her food to the back porch. Terry might see that as a slight, though.

She wanted her mother to be happy. Really, she did. But it was just so weird, seeing her with a man who wasn't PC's father. It was something she'd have to come to terms with. She knew that. Didn't make it easy. On the bright side, perhaps he and Rocky could help with the animals, and PC would feel comfortable going back home to Houston. But she didn't have a high degree of confidence in that at the moment. Or was she just making an excuse to stay in Possumwood?

"Cordie! Come on! My lunch is getting cold."

He looked up at her as if to say, "Are you talking to me?"

"Chicken jerky?"

Cordie snorted and bounded across the yard toward her.

PC shook her head. *If you can't beat 'em, bribe 'em.*

The payoff made, PC sat on the loveseat with her lunch special. The egg roll was still hot enough that she had to open her jaw wide and huff in air to keep it from scorching the roof of her mouth. She should probably have let Cordie have a little more turn-out time.

Rose scooped up a forkful of rice. "How's that case going?"

"Which one?" PC asked automatically.

"The one where Justice found the bones?"

PC nodded as she chewed. "Not a lot to go on. Hopefully, the forensic artist from DPS will get back with us soon with a render of their facial reconstruction."

Terry set his tea down. "Have you heard anything about the one they found in the well at the mayor's house?"

"Not yet. The tech told us that they did a 3D print of the skull and were doing the full clay reconstruction. Who knows, he might end up at the Quenton Plantation when it's all said and done."

"Wouldn't that beat all?" Rose speared a seared pineapple chunk.

Terry patted her thigh. "After the incident at the re-enactment last month, I've been spending some time at the library, trying to see what I could find. One thing is awful peculiar, though. That well at Phineas Scott's? It was a big disappointment. Dry as a bone. That big ole oak tree probably sucks up all the water. Well on the other side of the house was good, though."

"Huh. Seems weird they didn't fill it in." PC took the lid off her container of egg drop soup.

Terry shrugged. "They'd probably already used the dirt for something else."

"Good point." PC waved the remains of her eggroll.

The history talk had made PC eager to read some more of Mamie's journal, so as soon as she was done with her lunch, she retreated to her bedroom and opened the old diary.

October 28, 1851

Oh, most joyous of days! William has returned! He said that he had been out hunting for squirrels, or a good fat rabbit, when he became lost in the woods. There were acorns and pecans, and of course a few late persimmons, that he foraged to sustain himself. Mother could not refrain from embracing him at random intervals. After she had retired for the evening, he came

*into the parlor where I was carding cotton and
informed me that he had a secret. He would
show me tomorrow, when Mother was out at the
market.*

PC turned the page. There was nothing. This was the last entry in the diary. She picked up one of the other journals, but the first page was dated three months prior. The other two were even earlier. *Mamie! You had two blank pages left. You couldn't write the secret there? Does Justice have more of these lying around in her attic?*

When PC woke her phone to call Justice, she noticed she had some new emails, so she thought she'd check those first. One was from the DPS Forensic Art group. *Is this the John Doe render?*

She opened the email, skipping the text and waiting impatiently for the render to download. And then she almost dropped her phone.

Looking back at her was a near-perfect likeness of Dr. McIlwraith.

Chapter 9

PC BLINKED RAPIDLY and gave her head a shake. Dr. McIlwraith still stared from her phone. The color of his eyes was wrong, and his hair was darker. But it was him.

Who on earth would want to kill the State Archeologist? Should she call Dr. DuPree and offer condolences?

She decided against it—the anthropologist might not be aware of it yet. The detective made her way back to the Possumwood PD. Now, at least, there was a place to begin.

As soon as PC walked in the front door, Annie looked up and said, "PC! Did you see the render?"

"I did. Hard to believe, isn't it?"

"I never met him, but Hiro said he seemed really nice. I don't understand…" She shook her head and buzzed PC through the security door.

PC shrugged as she walked through. "Murder doesn't always make sense."

She looked around for Tran, but he wasn't in his cube, or visiting any of the workstations. She would text him later. Once she logged into the laptop, she opened her email and printed the render of Dr. McIlwraith. With the image in front of her, she started making a list of people who might have information on the doctor or his schedule the day he died.

Cooper Downing, number one. The assistant should be intimately familiar with his mentor's schedule. Even if he had no grievance against his boss, chances were that he knew about it if someone else did.

McIlwraith's co-workers. Had he been acting strangely? Said anything off? Gotten into any feuds?

People from the university where Downing was a grad student. How did he strike people? Any issues there?

She should probably ask Justice if she'd seen McIlwraith wandering around her property. PC chewed the inside of her cheek. Justice probably would have already brought that up. Did McIlwraith mention something in his Friday afternoon interview with her?

Was it worth contacting Dinah Mae Brown? There was a chance she'd have spoken with him about Mirabella County historical artifacts while he was in town. She'd be eager for any new exhibit-worthy items he uncovered in his dig.

Coffee. Better fill up my mug before I go out and start talking to people. I really should text Tran and see if he is available to go with me.

The security door clicked open and PC heard Tran's voice. "Ma'am. Please. Don't make this difficult."

"You have no right! I didn't do nothin'!"

PC hurried to the corridor and saw Tran coaxing a recalcitrant Justice toward the interview room.

"What's going on?"

Justice's head swiveled toward PC. "Thank goodness you're here! Can you talk some sense into this young fella?"

Tran breathed in deeply. "Ms. Johnson, we just want to ask you some questions. It's routine. We would interview anyone who found a body on their property, isn't that right, PC?"

"Of course. Justice, would you like me to come in and help?"

"Sure."

PC caught up with them and Tran unlocked the door to a small, grey room. She'd seen bigger walk-in closets. Justice sat down in a metal chair that was bolted to the floor at the far end. PC stood inside while Tran retrieved a plastic chair from down the hall, then gestured for PC to sit in it. She did, and he leaned against the closed door.

PC assumed there was a camera behind her, recording the interview, but she didn't look to verify it. Her knees were less than a foot from Justice's. PC smiled and breathed deeply.

"So, Justice, I'd like you to refresh my memory. Describe to me again how you found the body, um, bones."

Justice leaned back against her chair, her eyes dark. "For the umpteenth time, I scooped up the compost with the Bobcat and when I dumped it at the mushroom bunker, there it was."

"Okay. I noticed that your other compost piles were covered in tarps that were weighed down with blocks. Was that pile also covered that way?"

"Course it was."

"Okay. So when you were getting it ready to load, did you notice anything unusual? Anything out of place?"

"No." Justice chewed her lip. "Well. I didn't think much of it. I always put the cinderblocks flat side up. Two of 'em was hole side up. Thought I might've had a senior moment last time I turned the pile."

"Do you have many senior moments?" Tran asked, his voice earnest.

Justice shot him such a withering look that PC could feel him shriveling up behind her. *Don't antagonize the witness. Jeez.*

"Alright. That's fine. Two blocks were turned the wrong way."

Justice sat up straighter. "Can you dust 'em for prints?"

"That's an idea." *They'd all have to be sent to the lab for special latent print processing, and the techs might be able to pull something with fluorescent powder. And who knows if the unsub was wearing gloves?*

The goat farmer leaned forward, as if she were starting to get excited about helping with the case.

PC nodded reassuringly. "I'm sure Officer Tran will keep those possible fingerprints in mind as he goes through his investigation. But tell me about Dr. McIlwraith. How well did you know him?"

Justice's lip twitched. A micro-expression. Disgust?

"Not very well. Why would I know him? He only just came to town a few days ago."

"What kind of interactions did you have with him?"

There was a hard set to Justice's jaw now. "Well. He called me and asked a few questions, then he wanted me to come into town and meet with him. And bring the family Bible."

"Did you find the Bible?"

"Not for the meetin', no. I told you that."

"I know you did. I'm just trying to clarify everything for Officer Tran, so he knows exactly what's going on. It'll help him get to the bottom of this."

Justice's eyes drifted up to Tran and back down to PC. She crossed her ankles.

She doesn't want to talk with him in here. "Justice, would you like a coke?"

"Well, I am a bit parched."

"What kind do you want?"

"You got any Dr Pepper?"

PC turned and gave Tran a look.

"I can go check the machine," Tran said. "I think we have some, but it goes fast."

He left, and PC leaned forward. "Justice, what did Dr. McIlwraith say to you at the interview?"

"It was nonsense! Garbage!"

PC involuntarily pulled back, not expecting the outburst. "Can you clarify that?"

"He was tryin' to double check some ancestry stuff. That's why he wanted the Bible." Her eyes narrowed. "He had no right to try to drag my family's name through the mud."

"Really? What did he say?"

Justice leaned toward PC and replied in a harsh whisper. "You know those diaries I gave you? My great-great-great-great grandmother, Mamie Wharton? He said Hannah Justice was definitely her mother, but he didn't think Francois de Lamartine was her father." Her head shook, small back-and-forth motions. "You don't go trashin' people's folks around here, and—"

The door opened and Tran returned with a drink for Justice.

Really? PC glared at Tran. *Who taught you interrogation techniques?*

"Justice, I need to go to the ladies' room. Why don't you have your drink and relax for a minute?" PC got up and dragged Tran out of the room with her.

"Come with me," she hissed between her teeth as she turned toward the conference room.

Once they got there, she turned. "What were you thinking? Were you not listening outside, or watching the video?"

"What video?"

"You don't record interviews?"

"We have one of those little digital voice recorders, but it was out of battery."

What? PC felt like her eyes were going to pop out of her head from the increase in her blood pressure.

Tran shrugged. "Typically, we *may* bring three people a year in for questioning. Can't really justify a camera system."

PC rubbed her eyes. Justice was angry with Dr. McIlwraith. She didn't for a moment believe her mother's friend had killed the archaeologist over an alleged affair from more than a hundred years ago. And if she had, Justice had all the equipment to dispose of the body on her farm, and no one would ever know, so it made no sense that she would skeletonize the remains and then call PC.

She had to remind herself that murder didn't always make sense.

"Justice had an argument with McIlwraith, and she was telling me about it. Then you interrupted. I'll have to start all over. Why don't you just cut her loose, and I'll go by her house tomorrow and talk to her some more."

"Can't do that."

"Why not?"

"Chief thinks she did it. Wants her held, while we try to turn something up. He's pretty sure we can, now that the victim's been identified."

PC's shoulders sagged. "Don't you think, if she really did commit the murder, that it would be better to release her and observe what she's doing and where she's going? There was no evidence found at the scene."

Tran sighed. "It isn't my call."

"Let me go back in and talk to her."

He nodded.

"But I am going to the bathroom first."

PC knocked on the interrogation room door before she entered. "Hey, Justice. Officer Tran tells me the Chief is concerned about you being out on the farm all by yourself." *And destroying evidence.* "So, he wants to keep you in custody, just for a little bit, in case the killer panics and comes back to your place to clean up anything he left behind." PC had lied to plenty of suspects before. But never to a friend. She tasted bile rising in her throat, slimy and bitter.

"But my animals!" Justice stood up.

"I'll take care of them." PC pulled out her notebook. "Write down the feeding instructions."

The pen scratched on the paper as Justice wrote. Was it always so loud in here? Or was it guilt eating away at PC? Would her lie be found out? They couldn't hold Justice for more than seventy-two hours, not without charging her, and they didn't have a bee's fart worth of evidence. She also didn't think anything she could say or do would change Woody's mind. Except find the actual killer.

Justice handed the pen and notebook back to PC. "Gate code's on there, but you'll need the keys to get in the house." She reached into her pocket and handed them over.

"Don't you worry. I'll get everyone taken care of." PC noted the name scrawled at the bottom of the page.

"Who's that?"

"My lawyer, in case Elwood Wilson's got any crazy ideas."

Too late for that.

After she left the interrogation room, she found Tran. "I have her keys so I can feed her animals. I told her that she was here for her own protection. She'll probably be more cooperative if you let her keep thinking that, instead of treating her like a criminal."

"How do you know she's not?"

PC wanted to say, "Because I know her. I've seen her with her animals. She wouldn't hurt a flea." But she also knew that under the right circumstances, anyone could kill.

"I don't. But ask yourself: Does it make any sense that she would have killed McIlwraith, flensed him, and called the cops when she could have used her farm equipment to bury him out in the back forty?"

"Hmmm."

PC waved the Moleskine. "Now, if it was up to me, I'd canvass the neighbors and find out if any of them saw something out of place, or someone that didn't belong."

"What are we waiting for?"

Chapter 10

TRAN KNOCKED ON the front door of Melvin Stewart, the cousin who lived across the street from Justice. A small dog barked. Moments later, the door cracked open, the security chain taut.

"Can I help you?" asked the woman peering through the gap. She was younger than PC, but she wasn't exactly a spring chicken.

"Yes, ma'am. I'm Officer Tran, Possumwood PD. This is Detective Donovan. We'd like to ask you a few questions."

The woman crossed her arms. "I never seen that road construction sign. I swear. I wondered why everybody was goin' so slow."

PC pulled out her notebook and put on a smile. "Anybody could make that mistake. We aren't here to chase you down for a traffic violation. Not at all." She shook her head ever so slightly. "Just for my records, who do we have the pleasure of speaking with?"

"Merrilyrow."

"I'm sorry? Would you mind spelling that for me?"

"M-A-R-Y then L-E-E then R-O-W-E."

"Great. Thank you, Mary Lee. May we come in?"

Tran shifted his weight. "What we were wondering is whether you or anybody else here happened to notice anything, or anyone, out of the ordinary across the street last weekend?"

"At Justice's? You mean aside from all them cop cars?"

"Yes, ma'am." The young officer gave a quick nod.

Mary Lee pushed the door closed, and PC heard the chain end being slid down the track. The door opened again, this time all the way. "Y'all come on in. This is about them bones, isn't it?"

A tan chihuahua wearing a pink rhinestone collar growled and barked at them. Mary Lee scooped her up. "Puddin' you be nice to the po-lice, now."

Tran and PC followed Mary Lee into the living room, and she directed them to a threadbare beige and brown plaid sofa. An off-brand flat screen TV blared a black and white movie PC didn't recognize. A man who looked to be around seventy stared at it, a can of beer sitting in the cup holder of his recliner.

Mary Lee picked up the remote. "Daddy, I need to pause your movie for a minute." The scene froze. Melvin didn't seem to notice. "I'll just get my husband." She gave PC and Tran a lopsided smile. "Dallas!" Mary Lee bellowed. "Get in here."

Puddin' barked again.

Dallas sauntered into the room. His greasy, dishwater blond hair was slicked back, the ends brushing the top of his collar. The first two buttons of his pale blue Oxford shirt were missing, revealing a greyish undershirt.

"Sorry, Marely. Just managin' my inventory."

PC took a subtle breath through her nose. No pungent smell of pot plants nor any solvent or sulfur smell of a meth lab.

Mary Lee's eyes flashed. "Yeah, well you need to move some of that inventory. That's the third program you signed up for since Christmas, and you ain't sold none of that other crap, neither."

Dallas got a look on his face. PC wasn't sure if it was inspiration or a psychotic break. He trotted off down the hall and came back a few moments later, a large pill bottle in each hand. With a grin, he gave one to Tran and one to PC.

"Y'all must get real tired, doin' all that po-licin'. Lotta work, that job. And I got just the thing! These here vitamins will give you more energy than the entire oil patch in Texas." He tapped the lid of one jar with a dirty fingernail. "And they're made right here in the good ole US of A."

"That," PC exchanged a glance with Tran, "is awfully kind of you, Dallas, to be so considerate of our wellbeing. Really thoughtful. But the thing is, as investigators, we're not allowed to, you know, have any financial relationship with witnesses. I'm sure those vitamins are really great, though."

Dallas' face fell as Tran set his bottle down on the wobbly coffee table, next to a battered copy of Dale Carnegie's *How to Win Friends and Influence People*. PC felt sorry for the would-be entrepreneur. He wasn't the first sucker snagged by a multi-level marketing scheme.

"I tell you what. Do you have a card? Maybe when the investigation is over, I can give you a call. These things do take a while to wrap up, though."

"Yes, ma'am."

He dug in the pocket of his well-worn khakis and pulled out a business card. It must have come with the vitamins, because it had the brand name and logo printed in glossy ink, with blank lines for his name and phone number. He picked up a ballpoint pen from the coffee table, hastily filled it in, then proudly handed it over to PC.

"Thank you." She tucked the card into a small pocket in the cover of her notebook.

"Alright." Tran fidgeted with his duty belt. "As you may be aware, there was an incident across the street at Justice Johnson's place Sunday morning."

"You mean them old bones she found with the tractor?" Dallas ran his tongue along his teeth.

"Yes. The skeleton. Did anybody see anything unusual over the weekend? Hear anything out of place? Any of your neighbors acting strange?"

Melvin continued staring at the motionless scene on the television. Dallas scratched his chin.

"Well," Mary Lee started. "There was somethin'. Probably don't mean nothin'." She shook her head.

"Maybe. Maybe not." PC did her best to sound encouraging. "You just never know when some tiny piece of information will break the case wide open. What was it that you saw?"

Mary Lee hugged the dog to her chest. "Well, Saturday night, I guess it was Sunday mornin' though. Anyway, Puddin' started barkin' up a storm. I remember it was 3:02 on the clock. I tried to get her to go out and pee-pee, but she wouldn't, so I figured it must have been a coyote or somethin' like that. Justice's dogs was also barkin'."

"Did you see or hear anything aside from the dogs?"

"Nah. Me and Puddin' went out back in the little yard, but that's facin' away from Justice's place."

"Thanks, Mary Lee. How about you, Dallas? Did you notice anything?" PC hoped that taking his card would have put them on good enough terms that he'd be willing to offer a quid pro quo.

"I didn't even wake up for the dog. Sorry."

"It's okay. So, last week, or even the week before, have any of your neighbors done anything unusual? Had you spoken to Justice?"

"I saw her at the mailbox Thursday. Or was it Wednesday? I'm not sure. Anyway, she was all excited about getting' some kind of fancy long-haired goats." Dallas shrugged. "But she didn't seem no different from usual."

PC turned to Mary Lee.

She shook her head. "I didn't see nothin' unusual."

The detective gave her a little nod. "Officer Tran will leave you his card, in case you remember anything. Thank you for speaking with us." PC stood up, and Tran followed her lead.

They drove to the Gunnersons' place. It was easy to recognize because not only was there a big 'G' on the gate, but there was a he-lipad near the entrance. They used the intercom attached to a large solar panel, but the housekeeper told them her employers were away—they'd been in Europe for the past two weeks and weren't expected back for another few days. She didn't live on the premises and was only there during the day.

Tran made a U-turn, and they drove back up the road to the Turners' farm. A wooden sign on thick posts announced that they had arrived at

FARO FARMS

ORGANIC VEGETABLES ✦ EXOTIC FRUITS ✦ HERBS

JAMAAL TURNER, PROPRIETOR.

Green, yellow, and red stripes bordered the sign. A man in a plaid shirt with the sleeves rolled up was working in a raised bed in the front yard. He stood and dusted off his hands as the squad rolled up his driveway.

PC got out of the car. "Afternoon. Are you Mr. Turner?"

The man wiped sweat off of his forehead with his arm and brushed a dreadlock out of his eyes. "Who's asking?"

"I'm Officer Tran, Possumwood PD, and this is Detective Donovan. We're investigating the incident down the street from you—"

"At Justice's place? She told me about that. Crazy, huh?"

PC moved around the car, so she was a bit closer and didn't feel like she was shouting at the witness. "Do you know her pretty well?"

"Reasonably well. Why?"

"We've been checking with the neighbors to see if anybody saw or heard anything unusual last weekend. Did you or your wife see anything strange? Or anyone acting out of character?"

"Teskia was in Austin at a craft show. She left Thursday night and didn't get back until Monday morning. I'd been building some more raised beds in the back on Saturday, and I slept like a rock that night. I don't remember anything off on Friday or Sunday. Except when all the cops showed up."

"Justice told me your wife does stained-glass and pottery. Did she have a booth at Maifest? I saw some gorgeous pieces there." PC noted a rusty stain on the white fieldstone that made up walls of the raised bed.

"She sure did. I'll tell her you liked them."

"Your wife is very talented." PC gestured to the stone structure. "Is this bed you're working in new?"

Turner shook his head. "No. But I'm topping off the soil and adding fertilizer."

"Those plants sure do look lush. They must be happy with whatever you're feeding them."

Tran handed Mr. Turner his card. "Thanks for taking a minute to talk with us. If you remember anything, please give me a call."

"Will do."

The farmer stood and watched as they backed out of his driveway.

Tran paused at the road. "What now?"

"I told Justice I'd feed her goats, so we may as well do that since we're here, then we can go talk to the neighbor that backs up on her property." She consulted her notebook. "Ben Masters."

"Sounds good."

PC set her notebook in her lap. "Did you notice anything odd at Turner's place?"

"Odd? Not really. It was kind of stinky, but he did say he was fertilizing."

"Yeah. But there was something that looked like it might have been a bloodstain on the side of the bed."

"What? Why didn't you say something?"

"I just did."

"We should go back and ask him to dig up the bed."

"You don't have a warrant and you don't have a strong case for probable cause. It could be a rust stain for all I know. But it's certainly worth keeping on the radar. Definitely look into Turner's background."

Tran huffed out a breath and drove to Justice's. They made their way up the caliche road to the gate, and PC gave him the code. Now there was a song stuck in PC's head. *Row, row, row your boat, gently down the stream. Merrily, merrily, merrily, life is but a dream...* Feeding the goats might banish it.

There was no direct route to get to the road that gave access to the land on the other side of Justice's farm, and they had to go some way down the road before they could cut across to the parallel lane. But they finally found Ben Masters' driveway. Yaupon bushes and cedar trees obscured the view to the property, but there was an ordinary corrugated aluminum gate, left half open, in the drive. PC got out and opened it the rest of the way, then pushed it closed after Tran drove through.

Between the shrubbery, the roll of the land, and the curve of the road, the house wasn't visible until they were almost right on it. It was nothing fancy—a single-story log cabin-style structure. Justice was right about the solar panels. Masters had a whole solar farm going.

They got out of the car and headed toward Masters' front door. PC grabbed Tran by the back of his collar and pulled him up short.

"What are you doing?" he growled as he straightened his shirt.

PC pointed to the gravel walkway. "That's a tripwire."

Chapter 11

TRAN LOOKED DOWN at the thin cord, almost the same color of the caliche walkway, only inches from his ankle. "IED?"

"I don't know if it's an explosive or a doorbell. Just go carefully and watch for booby traps." PC scanned the area, looking for anything that might spring up and fly at them.

Tran stepped over the wire, and PC followed cautiously. A concrete patio, covered by a stained and dusty fabric awning, ran along the entire front of the cabin. A railing at the edge of the awning was lined with plastic window boxes. Basil, oregano, dill, sage, and parsley tumbled over the edges of the planters and stretched toward the sun. A fist-sized Zuni bear fetish, carved out of obsidian, or possibly onyx, guarded a clump of thyme. A jagged arrow, made of inlaid turquoise and trending upward, graced one side of the bear.

Tran knocked on the storm door of the cabin.

"What do you want?" The voice came from a video doorbell system protected by a metal cage.

"Officer Tran, Possumwood PD. And Detective Donovan. We'd like to ask you some questions about last weekend."

"What about it?"

PC stepped closer to the camera. She was hoping for a window in the entry door so she could get a glimpse inside the house, but the door behind the storm door appeared to be reinforced steel. There were some models that looked like standard issue front doors, but he hadn't sprung for that. *Was it a budgetary constraint, or did he want people to be aware they were facing a secured entry?* "Hello? Mr. Masters? Sorry to bother you—I'm sure you're very busy. We were just wondering if you noticed anything out of the ordinary, or any people you hadn't seen before at Ms. Johnson's place."

There was no response.

PC was just about to try talking to the doorbell again, when the steel door opened. A man in olive drab combat fatigues pushed open the storm door as he pulled the steel one closed behind him. His dirty hair looked like he probably cut it himself, and a scraggly, uneven beard clung to his jaw like fuzzy mold on bread. PC and Tran had to step back to avoid being knocked over.

"Why do you think I might have seen anything?" Masters tapped his thigh with an index finger.

Is he armed? A knife strapped to his ankle? His wrist? A handgun in his back waistband? Why all the security? The first thing that popped into her head was 'meth lab,' but no noxious miasma had seeped from the door.

"Mr. Masters?" She gave him a second to react to the name. "We're talking to everybody. So far, we've been at the Turners' and Melvin Stewart's place." She picked up the Zuni bear. "This is a beautiful piece. Where did you get it? My mama collects things like that." *Rose collects just about anything.*

Masters took a step forward, his right hand reaching for the medicine bear. PC put it back where she'd found it, and his hand dropped to his side.

"Sedona. Got it in Arizona." His Adam's apple bobbed. "I didn't notice nothin' out of place over the weekend."

"Oh. Okay." PC gave him the friendliest smile she could muster. "Thanks for speaking with us. If you remember seeing or hearing anything, please call Officer Tran down at the station."

Tran handed over a card, and Masters snatched it.

"I told you, I didn't see nothin'." He turned and slipped back inside his house.

Tran started to speak, but PC raised her hand to quiet him. They picked their way back to Tran's squad, searching for tripwires and traps. Once they were inside, he said, "That was the shortest interview I've ever heard of. What was even the point of talking to him, if that was all you were going to ask?" He started turning the car around.

PC pulled out her notebook. "Did he have a weapon?"

"I didn't see one."

"Exactly. But there was a tripwire, a reinforced door, and a very nervous witness. Why do you think someone might have a tripwire on their front walkway? A steel door?"

"They're up to something sketchy."

"Ding, ding, ding. We have a winner."

Tran stopped the car and PC got out to open the gate.

She wiped her hands on her pants when she got back in the car. "Now, I think it would be safer for everybody to start with a background investigation of this jumpy neighbor. Are there any complaints about him? Does he have a record? Did he know Dr. McIlwraith? I would say pull his utilities and see how much power he goes through, but with that solar array, he's probably off the grid. You can be looking into all that while I go talk to Phineas Scott."

Anubis sat by his owner's chair, the canine's black skin shining in the sunlight that filtered through the large windows. His yellow eyes were saturnine orbs of disapproval. Dogs usually liked PC, but this one seemed to be the exception.

Phineas Scott took a swig of his drink. "I was shocked when the Rangers showed up at my door and told me that the bones Justice found on Sunday belonged to Dr. McIlwraith. They looked around for a while at the archaeological dig, then left."

"Do you know if Dr. McIlwraith had found any more artifacts?"

"He hadn't mentioned any, but I didn't necessarily see him every day."

"Did you ever get a chance to ask Dinah Mae at the Historical Society about those old keys that got stolen in your break-in last month? I believe there was a silver one missing. The others were laying in the water. I wondered if that particular one had fallen into the bushes, or perhaps slid to the deep end of the pond."

The mayor rubbed Anubis' ears. "No. It didn't turn up. So weird that somebody would break into my house to steal a key for a lock that hasn't been used in a hundred years. I did ask her about it, though. Dinah Mae didn't know anything about the keys."

"It's even weirder that someone would kill the State Archaeol-ogist and try to pass off his remains as an artifact."

"True." He took another sip of his drink. "I liked Dr. McIlwraith, and it's terrible what happened to him. But I won't be sad when this archaeological dig is over. I wonder if his assistant is going to finish it up?"

PC shifted in her chair. "Cooper Downing? I have no idea how project succession works in the State Archaeology Department. But speaking of Downing, what did you think of him? Did he and McIlwraith get along?"

"As far as I could tell. Downing seemed like an excitable fellow, though. A few times I saw him and Dr. McIlwraith talking. Downing was waving his arms around like some demented windmill, but nobody was yelling. His boss just stood there listening, so I never knew what all that was about. Like I said earlier, they've found a couple of little things, but nothing significant."

PC let her eyes drift to Anubis. "I bet it was trickier letting your dog out to do his business with all the official stuff going on."

Phineas snorted. "No, not tricky at all. I'm not allowed to let Nubie out there. I couldn't even let my friends in the back yard—I had to cancel a barbecue *and* a margarita party."

His lips pursed together, and PC wondered what words he was holding back.

She nodded sympathetically. "Must have been really frustrating. Did they give you a time frame from when they might be finished with the dig?"

The mayor's drink sloshed out a little on the end table as he slammed it down. "Of course not! That would be too simple. They have to sift through dirt a cup at a time, fill out reports, take pictures. I think they even had a drone one day. Apparently, they've applied for permission to use ground penetrating radar. Who knows if and when that'll get approved? The bureaucracy must interfere with people's everyday lives as much as possible."

The detective gave a sympathetic smile. "They don't give you special scissors to cut through red tape when you're the mayor?" *And part of the local bureaucracy.*

"I wish they did."

PC stood up. "Thanks for taking the time to talk with me. Hope they get your back yard taken care of soon. If you happen to see Cooper Downing, could you give me a call?"

Phineas cocked his head. "Do you think...?"

"No more than anybody else. Just talking to everybody right now. I'm sure the Chief will be working with the Rangers on this. We'll get to the bottom of it, one way or another." PC studied his face for a reaction, but nothing seemed out of place.

Phineas stood up to walk her to the door. "I wish they'd never found that old skeleton in my well last month. This seems to have stirred up a hornets' nest."

"Who knows? It may be Francois de Lamartine himself. There could really be a lost treasure after all."

"Or maybe McIlwraith found it, and that's why he was killed."

"Perhaps."

PC could feel the glaring yellow eyes of Anubis all the way back to her car and she was glad to pull out of the drive and get on the road. It was long past lunchtime, and she was starved. A bite and a cup of java at the City Café? She looked at her FlitBit—six minutes to get there before closing. Looked like the Brisk Rib instead.

The lunch crowd was long gone and only a few tables were occupied. PC got her usual, the Brisk Tater #3, and some tea.

"Hey, Primrose!"

Thorne Marberger waved from a corner table. She walked over to join him–she'd been planning on talking to him, anyway. Had Dr. McIlwraith perhaps strayed onto Thorn's ranch and had an encounter with the angry rancher? Or his one-ton bull?

She pulled out a chair. "You slummin', Thorne?"

"Ha! I was down at the courthouse having a talk with Travis Bailey, and it ran longer than I expected."

PC sat down. "You trying to strong-arm the DA into pressing more charges against those treasure hunters on your ranch?"

An eyebrow arched on his wide forehead. "Someone could have been killed when they let my cattle out. Not to mention property damage to my livestock. Those boys need to learn a lesson."

She made a noncommittal noise and took a drink of her tea. "Did you ever talk to the State Archaeologist, Dr. McIlwraith?"

"Why do you ask?

"He'd been interviewing people around town—he talked to Justice on Friday."

"Well, I was in Houston all week. Got back Sunday just in time to round up my cows. Haven't talked to anybody. If he finds the Lamartine treasure, he just might discover it's really the Marberger treasure."

"But he never came out to your ranch?" PC watched his face carefully.

Thorne shook his head. "Not as far as I know. But I hope he wouldn't take it upon himself to do his archaeology-ing on my property without permission. But who knows? I guess he'll call me next week if he wants to come out."

PC's McIlwraith vs Marberger theory fell apart like a milk-sodden cookie. Thorne didn't appear to be aware the archaeologist was dead, for one thing. He said he'd been out of town, and the killer spent a lot of time processing his victim—commuting an hour each way between Possumwood and Houston for such an act was probably not feasible.

She pried off a bit of potato from the freakishly large spud on her plate. "So, you haven't heard, then."

"Heard what?"

"Dr. McIlwraith is dead."

"What?" His plastic tea glass stopped halfway to his mouth.

"He was found at Justice's place Sunday morning."

Thorne frowned. "I thought... I mean Sylvia had said Justice had dug up some old bones with her backhoe."

"Technically, it was a Bobcat. But the bones she found weren't old, just made to look that way."

"Why would someone do that?"

"Why, indeed? That's one of the many questions we're trying to answer."

Thorne set his glass down and pushed his chair back from the table, leaving about a third of his sandwich on the plate. "I gotta run, Primrose. It was good seeing you. Good luck figuring all this out."

A cowbell clattered as the door bumped shut behind him. PC dug into her potato and chewed thoughtfully. Who had a reason to kill the archaeologist? No one, so far. Who would benefit from his death? Possibly Cooper Downing, but that wasn't certain. There was no obvious reason for his murder. Not yet, at least. PC needed to get her hands on the list of people he'd interviewed last week. Something might turn up then. What if… it was an accident? The murder wasn't intentional, but somebody panicked and tried to cover up McIlwraith's death? That was a whole other can of worms that PC may very well have to open.

PC drank the last of her tea and cleaned up her table.

Would Dinah Mae Brown at the Historical Society be privy to any discoveries Dr. McIlwraith had made?

Chapter 12

PC GOT INTO her car and headed toward the Quenton Plantation. During the drive, she tried to still the thoughts jumbling around in her head. She had questions—so many questions—but no answers. If she could stop worrying the problem like a terrier, it might help some connections form or ideas bubble to the surface. So, she stared straight ahead at the road and almost missed the driveway.

When she arrived at the ticket window, a young man wearing a brocade vest and a striped cotton shirt gave her a wink and a grin. "That'll be ten dollars, please, miss."

"Actually, I'm here to see Ms. Brown. Is she in?"

"Who should I tell her is calling?"

"Detective Donovan."

The man made a phone call. When he hung up, he said, "She's in the second-floor parlor."

"Thanks."

PC made her way up the marble staircase and found Dinah Mae standing in front of a display case with a bar-code scanner in one hand. A laptop computer rested on the floor nearby and a metal cart loaded with artifacts stood behind it.

She looked up as PC approached. "I'm changing out some of our exhibit pieces. We try to adjust the items to fit with the seasons."

"Seems like a good idea. Got to keep things fresh. I was wondering. Did you happen to speak with Dr. McIlwraith about his dig? Did he find anything?" PC's hand rested on the glass display case.

Dinah May scratched her nose. "He did stop by one day to look at some artifacts."

"Which artifacts?"

"I don't really recall." Dinah Mae swallowed hard, then closed her laptop and set the barcode scanner on top of it.

"It would really help if we had some idea what he was looking into."

"Why don't you ask him, then?"

PC locked eyes with the director. "You haven't heard?" PC paused as the director shook her head. "I'm sorry to tell you—he's deceased."

Dinah Mae's hand flew to her mouth. "What?"

"The bones found Sunday at Justice Johnson's? They belonged to Dr. McIlwraith."

"I... I had no idea." Dinah Mae's eyes rested on the case beneath PC's hand. "I had nothing to do with it."

What? "I never said you did."

The curator's eyes flashed. "But you're here talkin' to me aren't you?" She sighed. "I'm really sorry to hear about Dr. McIlwraith. He was a good man. I have to get back to my exhibits." She snatched up the barcode reader and opened the laptop.

What are you hiding, Dinah Mae? PC looked down at the case. It was the same set of dueling pistols she'd seen before. Small, mahogany handled. Bullet molds, packing rod, patches, and lead balls, all nestled into their own green velvet compartments. The museum tag said it belonged to Francois Lamartine in the 1840s.

"Dinah Mae? What—"

"It wasn't my fault!" A sob wracked her body.

"What wasn't your fault?"

"He knew. I don't know how, but he knew!"

PC forced herself to stay calm. "What did he know?"

Dinah Mae pulled a tissue from her pocket and wiped her nose. "The pistols. He knew about the pistols." She began to cry again.

"Okay. It's all right. Tell me what happened."

The curator sniffled. "Ted came to see me about a display. It was a series of keys in the shadow box at the Lamartine home, but I told him it was done before I ever worked here, and I didn't know anything about it."

"Okay. Please continue."

"He seemed agitated. When he passed by the pistols, he stopped and had a good look. Then he turned and yelled at me. Said they were fake." Her voice broke, and she sobbed a few times.

"And then what?"

"He was right."

"Okay."

Dinah Mae dabbed her eyes. "Lamartine's pistols were at an auction house. I didn't have anything like the budget, but the board of directors was keen to get them. But not keen enough to cough up the cash. Thorne Marberger could certainly have made a generous donation to the museum, if it was so important to acquire them. Sadly, he couldn't be bothered with that, even with all his bluster. In the end, I found a similar set, but the case was in much worse condition. Of course, that meant it was in my price range. I had to restore it myself before it could be displayed. They are authentic 1840s dueling pistols. They just didn't belong to Francois Lamartine."

"What did he say about them? Any idea why he was angry?"

"No. He just yelled about them being fake."

Doesn't seem to be a motive for murder here, but this has to mean something. "Thanks for sharing with me."

Dinah Mae sniffled. "I could have said they were pistols from the same era, even if they weren't his actual pistols. But everybody was so excited to have them. I didn't have the heart to disappoint anybody."

"I understand. That's a lot of pressure. I won't tell anybody, but you might want to change the label."

Dinah Mae nodded.

"Alright. I'll leave you to your displays. Please call me if you think of anything else." PC started to turn, then stopped. "You mentioned the shadow box with the keys. Is there anyone in the historical society or at the museum who might have information about those?"

"I'm not sure. I don't think so, though. If I remember correctly, they pulled all those locks off in the 1920s or 30s. Not sure when the key display was created. I can ask, but the person who'd really know..." she wiped her eyes. "... would be Tom Wharton."

Figures. "I'm sorry for your loss."

Dinah Mae's shoulders drooped. "I can't believe he's gone. I just went into his office the other day to tell him something..." Tears welled up in her eyes.

"The car accident was so unexpected. You have my condolences."

PC had just started her car when her text chime sounded. She almost ignored it, then noticed it was from Tran.

"Cooper Downing making a statement. You might want to hear this."

Chapter 13

PC DROVE TO downtown Possumwood as fast as she dared. She almost waved to one officer parked on the shoulder on the downward slope of a rolling hill, lying in wait for speeders. Even though she was working on cases for the PPD, she doubted Woody would cut her any slack on a traffic ticket.

What was Cooper Downing up to? Where had he been? PC's foot itched to push the pedal harder.

It felt like hours before she finally pulled up in front of the station. Annie was working the desk and buzzed her through the security door.

She followed the sound of voices and found Hiro Tran and Erin Sanchez sitting at the conference table, across from Cooper Downing. PC watched discreetly from the doorway.

"I'm just telling you what I saw." Downing shook his head.

"Thank you for coming in to make a statement," Sanchez replied. "They'll have it typed up for you soon, and you can sign it and be on your way."

"Should have typed it up myself," he grumbled, eyes boring into the table.

"Henrietta is a very fast transcriptionist." Sanchez reassured him.

"Oh, hey!" PC said, as if she'd been walking by and noticed that Downing was in the conference room. "I'm sorry for your loss, Mr. Downing."

He peered up at her, barely raising his head, then mumbled something. PC assumed it was 'thank you.' She gave him a half-smile. "I know you've been through a terrible shock, but I would like to ask you some questions."

"Like what?" he snapped.

PC pulled out a chair on the same side of the table as Downing and sat down. "Do you have a minute? I was wondering about the dig. Had you and Dr. McIlwraith found any artifacts?"

He brightened a little at the mention of the archaeological pit. "We found a button and two coins from the 1840s."

"And where were those?"

"I don't remember the exact grid, but they were near the patio."

"And what about the well? Had you already investigated that?"

Downing scowled. "No. At least not together, anyway. Dr. McIlwraith was 'saving the best for last,' he said. I hadn't been down there, but I suspect *he* had."

"Why is that?"

"He always wanted to change the subject whenever I brought it up. Just said it was the icing on the cake."

PC drummed her fingers on the table. "He went down there when the skeleton was discovered."

Downing shrugged and shifted his knees away from PC. "As I told your friends, he and Justice Johnson got into a knockdown drag out when she came to be interviewed. Perhaps you should talk to her."

"I will. Of course, I will. What were they fighting about?"

"I didn't hear most of it. But he was going to ask her for a DNA sample. He had a theory—"

PC's brow crinkled. "I know. He thought that Francois de Lamartine wasn't actually her great-whatever grandfather. She was none too pleased about that. But I thought she already gave a sample to Dr. DuPree."

"Yeah?" Downing shrugged. "Different agency. Maybe he didn't have access to the results." He traced small circles on the table with his index finger. "He'd been studying some archival photos, and he claimed that she looked more like Mux Marberger than Francois." Downing shook his head. "He really wanted that family Bible, though. Which was weird, because who'd write that down? Especially in the Bible."

"I agree. But family is really important out here. Surely you could see how Dr. McIlwraith telling her that her nth grandmother was illegitimate would rile her up?"

"I suppose."

PC leaned her elbow on the table and held Downing's eyes. "Given how important your job helping Dr. McIlwraith was, I'm surprised you took a vacation at the same time he did. I would have thought you'd keep on working at the dig."

Downing's cheeks reddened. "I'd planned to. But Dr. McIlwraith texted me on his way out of town and told me to take the week off. Jerk. He should have told me earlier so I could have made plans."

"And about what time did he message you?"

Downing raised his hands, palms up. "It was getting dark. Maybe eight? I tried calling him back a little later, after I'd calmed down to see if I could get him to reconsider. That was about 9:30, but he never picked up."

Was it because he was dead?

Everyone jumped as Tran's phone vibrated on the table. He looked at it. "Your statement's ready. I'll go get it."

Downing nodded.

PC chewed on the inside of her cheek. She'd seen pictures of Mux Marberger. Justice didn't look much like him, although those genes must have been diluted after all this time. But there was something wrong with Downing's statement. PC just couldn't put her finger on it. Yet.

"And where did you see them arguing?"

"Where?"

"Yes."

Downing's eyes darted around the room. "It was... it was at the dig site."

Lack of corroborating witnesses is handy.

"She said he'd best let sleeping dogs lie, or else."

Pretty vague threat. "I see."

Tran returned with the typed statement. "Please read through it. If everything is correct, sign and date it."

Downing started to read, and PC got up. They were all in what passed for her office, but she couldn't really hang around and work while he was there. May as well go get a cup of coffee.

"Really?" PC frowned at the overflowing trash can beside the coffee maker. She had a few minutes to kill, and the garbage had the remains of someone's tunafish sandwich right on top, stinking up the tiny break room. PC gathered the edges of the trash can liner and eased it out of the bin, careful not to spill coffee grounds and noisome scraps on the floor as she tied up the opening. There was a dumpster out back. The door would lock behind her, and she'd have to come back around the front.

She carried her fetid burden down the hall and out the back door. As she stepped over to the dumpster, movement caught her eye.

"Is someone there?" Adrenalin set butterflies flapping in her stomach and electricity crawling over her skin. She took one step closer. "Hello?"

A metallic rattle came from behind the dumpster. A man stepped into view, dragging a trash bag.

"Mr. Masters? Is there something I can help you with?"

"No!" He looked at his boots, then back at PC's face, locking eyes with her. "I'm just collecting the aluminum cans you guys threw away. It's perfectly legal. Besides, the Chief said I could."

"It's okay. You just startled me. That's all." PC raised the trash bag. "I don't know if there are any cans in here, but it's pretty nasty. You may want to skip it." She pitched it into the open dumpster. "I'll leave you to your foraging. Have a nice day."

PC walked around to the front door. Her mind flew back to the day of the parade. She'd seen what appeared to be a homeless man in the alley way when the floats were lining up. But he wasn't Ben Masters. It was the longest of shots, but maybe she should try to track that man down to ask if he'd seen anything.

Annie gave her a double take. "How did…?"

"Took out the trash. So… Ben Masters was out there, rummaging through the garbage. Is that a normal thing?"

"Oh, sure. He shows up in town once a week, the day before the scrap buyer comes out to the junk yard, and collects cans and whatever metal he can get his hands on to sell."

"Heck of a way to make a living." PC paused. "Are there any other guys that you know of dumpster diving out there?"

Annie shook her head.

Cooper Downing gave her a curt nod as he came out of the security door and made for the exit. PC watched through the class door as he got into his car. There were certainly a number of people annoyed with Dr. McIlwraith, but who was angry enough to kill him?

Justice Johnson was upset because he was making insinuations about her 6th great-grandfather. Pretty flimsy reason to kill somebody.

Cooper Downing had some work-related friction. But this would be the first time she'd ever encountered a schedule change as a motive for murder.

Phineas Scott was frustrated with the archaeological dig in his back yard, but that was hardly the archaeologist's fault. And harming Dr. McIlwraith would extend the dig, not shorten it.

Dinah Mae Brown had mislabeled an artifact. She'd probably get scolded if it came out, but PC couldn't imagine her getting fired. It wasn't like people were clamoring for the job of Historical Society president and museum curator.

Thorne Marberger hated trespassers. And so did his bull, JoJo. Could there have been a fatal accident and coverup?

PC couldn't forget the rusty stain on the flowerbed stones at Justice's neighbor's house—Jamaal Turner. But she had no evidence that he'd ever even met Dr. McIlwraith.

Same with Ben Masters. He was an odd duck for sure, but was there a connection? Not that PC knew of. Same for the other man she'd seen in the alley.

Problem is, you don't know what you don't know. Were there any strangers in town? Any unknown subjects?

Then, of course, why were the bones found on Justice's farm? If Justice had killed him, she had the equipment to bury his body at the far end of her goat farm where no one would ever notice a fresh grave. It made no sense that she'd removed all but his bones and then called the police about it.

Was she being framed? If so, who would want to do that? None of PC's suspects had a strong motive for murder to begin with. Someone did, though. McIlwraith didn't bury himself in Justice's compost pile.

PC was vaguely aware of the security door behind her creaking open.

"Primrose? Would you mind giving me a ride home?"

Chapter 14

"WHAT?" PC TURNED to see Justice standing next to her.

"Woody told me that everything was secure, and I could go home."

What changed his mind? "Sure. Let me just get something. Be right back."

Annie buzzed PC through, and the detective headed straight to Tran's cubicle. He sat there, working on a report on his laptop.

PC cleared her throat as she came in. "Not that I'm complaining, but why did Woody cut Justice loose?"

He swiveled his chair around to face her. "You going to give her a ride?"

"Yes."

"Well, Dr. Mack believes that McIlwraith had to have been killed Friday night, probably before midnight. He thinks it would have taken hours to…uh…process the body, then the bones would need to dry most of the day Saturday before the dye would stick. As it turns out, Ms. Johnson was at a feed store just outside of Houston getting goat supplies. She said the local store was out of what she needed, so she had to drive almost into the city. On the way back, she stopped for dinner, then had a flat and called for roadside assistance. It was after one AM when she got home. She has the receipts."

"Huh." PC nodded. "I did tell you it wasn't her."

"I know."

The detective hurried out to the lobby. "Sorry about that. Let's go."

Justice settled into PC's SUV. "This sure is a fancy car. You got all the bells and whistles."

"Not quite all of them. I didn't think I needed the heated steering wheel."

"Yeah…if they'd just come up with a chilled steerin' wheel…"

PC pulled out of the parking lot. "Too true." She sped up to change lanes. "So. I've been having a really tough time finding anybody who might want to harm Dr. McIlwraith. Are you sure you haven't seen any strangers nosing around out at your farm?"

"As I told you before, no. The Turners sometimes have customers come to their place, and Teskia gets a lot of deliveries. The Gunnersons have guests once in a while, but they've been out of town. If there was anybody prowlin' 'round my property, the dogs would have run 'em off. That's their job—keepin' varmints out."

And yet, the bones still appeared.

"This is a tough one. Feels like there's a lot of information we just don't have."

"Your mama's always been proud a your detectin' skills. You'll figger it out."

"Hope you're right. I did feed everybody. Dogs are still penned up, though."

"Thank you for doin' that."

PC stopped for a traffic light. Dark clouds scudded along a fresh breeze. "Do you have any idea how often Jamaal Turner redoes the dirt in his flower beds? His plants sure look happy."

"Every spring. Mixes in a lot of bone meal and some other stuff. He helped me set up my mushroom growin' tables, you know. And blood meal. Can't use that on mushrooms, but he swears by it. Also keeps the deer and rodents away."

So much for that rusty stain. Probably is blood, just not likely to be McIlwraith's. The illumination on the instrument panel changed—the headlights had come on. *Hope we make it back to Justice's before the bottom falls out.*

"I saw Ben Masters a few minutes ago, collecting cans. Is that how he makes his living?"

Justice shrugged. "He mostly keeps to himself. He's got a motorcycle. A couple of times when the weather's been real bad, I've run him into town to pick up a prescription."

"Really? What for?" *Cholesterol? Anti-psychotic?*

"Didn't ask. Figgered that was his own private business. That boy don't talk much. But he does like his campfire. Sometimes, I can see one burning at his place at night, lotta times once or twice a week. Once a month or so, he and a couple of other fellas get out there with drums for an hour or two." Justice shook her head. "Keeps the goats stirred up until they quit."

Sheet lightning flickered through the clouds and thunder grumbled close behind it. PC drove a little faster.

"Do you think he's dangerous?"

Justice shrugged. "Not any more than anybody else."

There's a ringing endorsement.

"How were your dogs on Sunday?" *Could somebody have slipped 'em a mickey Saturday night?*

"Fine. Why?"

"Just trying to work out why they didn't go after whoever left the skeleton."

Justice shifted in her seat. "Well, they did bark some, in the middle of the night. But they huddled up on the porch. That only ever means one thing."

"What's that?"

"Feral hogs. They're meaner than all get out—they'll knock you down and eat you alive. Livin' or dead—they don't care. They'll eat anything. I stepped out on the porch with the dogs and could hear them hogs gruntin' and squealin' so I went back inside. The goats and donkeys are penned up at the barn at night when it's kid season, so I didn't worry none about them."

"Hmmm…"

The conversation drifted into silence as they neared the edge of town. PC kept an eye on the sky, willing the car to outrun the rain.

It was still dry when she came to a stop at the Capre Leche Farm gate. PC rolled down the window, and the restless air was probably twenty degrees cooler than when they'd left town. The detective punched in the gate code, drumming her fingers on the steering wheel as she waited for the motorized arm to swing the gate open.

Justice rested her arm on the side of the door. "Can you drop me at the barn? Got some pregnant does I need to check on."

"Sure."

"Thanks for the ride. I appreciate it. I'm havin' lunch with Elwood's mama tomorrow. She ordered a bunch of goatmilk soap. Maybe she can get that boy straightened out."

PC chuckled as she waved goodbye to Justice. Then she wondered if she had time to swing by Ben Masters' place before either he got back from his can collecting excursion or the sky opened up. Or both.

She made the trip somewhat faster than she should have, then parked on the grassy shoulder of the road just past the gravel driveway. The detective got out of the car. It had gotten so dark she'd need a flashlight for a quick look in the mailbox. No harm in that, was there? It wasn't like she was going to take anything. In the end, it didn't matter. Masters had a locking mailbox. There was, however, a cylinder on the side for newspapers. A rolled-up magazine took up most of the space. PC pulled it out. *The Psychonaut's Journey*. She flipped through it. Articles like "Magic Mushrooms = Anxiety Magic" and "Are You Really Ready for Ayahuasca?" sped by under her fingers.

Huh. She put the periodical back.

A glint of silver caught her eye. This time the gate had a padlock. She hadn't planned on going inside, anyway.

A fat drop of rain splattered onto her cheek. Then another. PC sprinted back to her car and made it inside with moments to spare as the heavens opened and rain bucketed down so hard she couldn't see five feet in front of her car. Hopefully Ben Masters wouldn't be riding home on his motorcycle in this torrent, because she'd have to wait for it to slack off before she could go anywhere. The detective yawned and noticed that she had a bad case of coffee breath. That made her think of the poster in the vet's office. *Master your dog's stinky breath with FreshBonz*. Master and bones were too close together for her comfort, reminding her that Ben Masters could very well be responsible for the bones in Justice's compost pile.

She considered her options. There wasn't enough probable cause to get a warrant to find out what prescription Masters took. He probably had means, and possibly opportunity, but if there was motive, PC couldn't see it.

Not for him or anybody else.

This case was stacking up to be uglier than homemade sin. A gruesome treatment of a corpse. No motive. No strong suspects. No trace evidence. Is that why the body was skeletonized, or was it to divert suspicion by disguising it as an antique? Or… was it a sick joke? Disguise the archaeologist as an artifact?

The torrent had slacked to merely hard rain. A jagged branch of lightning struck a tree with a blinding flash perhaps two hundred yards ahead, and the boom that followed rocked her vehicle. Seconds later, PC's phone rang.

"Justice?" Are you okay?"

"I need your help! It's an emergency. Get here as fast as you can."

The line went dead. PC dropped the phone onto the seat and grabbed the shifter.

She swore as she put the SUV into reverse and turned around in Masters' muddy driveway. What had happened to Justice? Had the hogs come back? Was she hurt? Dire possibilities ping-ponged around PC's head as she drove as fast as she dared in the pouring rain.

She pulled up at the barn, since that was the last place she'd seen Justice. Had she been trampled by a herd of eager goats?

"Justice!" PC called as she ran toward the goat pens.

"Here! In the barn!" came the reply.

"Are you okay? Do you need an ambulance?"

"No. Hurry up and get in here. Penelope needs your help!"

Penelope?

PC burst through the barn door to find Justice, wearing blue gloves that reached to her armpits, hugging a large brown and white goat around the waist.

"Grab her! Hold her up."

The detective did as she was told. Justice moved to the back end of the goat. "Baby's wrong. Have to move it, but she wouldn't quit layin' down."

The mama goat struggled against PC as Justice strained to re-position the kid. Finally, a greyish blue sack with legs sticking out of it plopped onto the straw. Justice tore at it, and the wet face of a baby goat came into view.

She shook the kid like a rag doll. "Breathe! Come on!"

Justice stopped shaking the goat for a moment.

Nothing.

She joggled the baby again.

Still nothing.

Justice put her mouth over its tiny snout and breathed air into its lungs three times. She pulled back.

The kid was still.

Finally, the tiny ribs expanded, and the little black goat let out a startled bleat.

The nanny goat knocked PC off her feet trying to free herself.

"Let Penelope go. She needs to tend her young 'un."

PC picked herself up and started to dust off her bottom, but found her hands were covered in goat blood, and some other substances that originated from places she'd rather not try to guess.

"There's a sink in the milkin' parlor. You can go get cleaned up. I got to do a couple of things here."

The detective smiled at the mama goat nuzzling her baby, who was looking surprised to be out of his former warm, dark home.

"What would you have done if I hadn't been close by?"

"Lost a kid. Possibly a goat. Jamaal Turner's helped me once or twice, but he wasn't pickin' up. Vet's thirty minutes away on a good day. Didn't think Penelope was gonna be ready to drop for another week."

"Glad I could help, but you scared me half to death when you said it was an emergency and then just hung up. I didn't know what to think."

"Sorry 'bout that. But I couldn't let Penelope lay down again."

PC nodded and left to clean her sticky hands. After a few wrong doors, she found the sink and scrubbed her filthy mitts. The pulsating fluorescent light revealed that goat goo was on more than just her hands. She'd have to borrow a towel from Justice so she didn't get it all over the seat in her car.

By the time she got back to the goat pen, the newborn had gotten to its feet and was aggressively nursing. Penelope stood with her eyes closed, and PC wondered if she was falling asleep after her ordeal.

The barn was lit for a moment by a flash of lightning. Thunder crackled, a little further away now, but it was still enough to make Penelope's eyelids snap open.

Justice peered out the door. "Gettin' dark. There's a break in the rain—we should probably make a run for it."

PC had parked near the barn, but there wasn't much use in getting in the car to drive less than a hundred feet to be nearer to the porch. They hurried to the house in the drizzle. Justice's dogs barked and jumped against their pen. One of them could almost clear the cyclone fence.

"Alright, I'm comin'." Justice veered toward the canines.

The dogs barked even more excitedly, and the smallest one began to bay. *Beagle mix, for sure.* Justice opened the gate, and the dogs spilled out like a handful of hairy bouncy balls. None of them jumped *on* Justice, but they danced around her and tried to lick her face, or wherever they could reach. She propped the gate open, so that they could shelter in their oversized doggie condo if the rain picked back up.

They lolloped in ragged circles around PC and Justice as the women made their way back to the house. Justice unlocked the door, and they stepped inside, the dogs making themselves comfortable on the veranda. She flipped on the lights and disappeared into the kitchen. Moments later, she returned with three dog bones. All three pups snapped to attention and sat politely the instant the screen door creaked. Each one got a treat. Thunder rumbled and the medium-sized dog tucked its tail and trotted to the dog pen, disappearing into the shelter. The beagle mix followed, at a much more leisurely pace. The huge fluffy grey dog sighed and picked up his bone, lumbering after his friends.

"Poor Joker." Justice closed the door behind her. "He's so scared of thunder. Don't bother Captain and Tipsy, but they go along for moral support, I guess. Now. Can I get you somethin' to drink?"

"Just a glass of water."

"Come on in the kitchen."

PC was reluctant to sit on anything, so she stood awkwardly in the middle of the room. Justice handed her some water from the fridge. Glancing through the window in the back door, PC could see the rain was starting to pick up again, so she swigged down about half of her drink in one gulp.

"If you're all right, then I'll head home. I still have Mama's animals to take care of. But if I could borrow a towel to sit on in the car, that'd be great."

A peal of thunder rattled the windows. Darkness swallowed the room.

Justice groaned. "Whatever they make them power lines out of, they need to try somethin' else. Almost every time it rains more than a half inch, the electricity goes out. Lemme get a flashlight."

PC stayed put while Justice rummaged around in a drawer. The detective thought she heard something on the back porch, but reasoned it was just the storm.

Until a flash of lightning revealed a man in a rain slicker standing at the door.

Ben Masters.

Is that a knife in his hand?

Chapter 15

PC DROPPED HER water. The plastic cup bounced off the wood floor, splashing liquid along the way. Justice whirled around, the beam of the flashlight glaring in Masters' face. He raised an arm to shield his eyes. There was indeed a large knife in his right hand.

"Drop it!" PC barked, although if he chose not to, there was precious little she could do about it.

He raised the blade.

PC backed up, pulling Justice with her.

Justice lowered the flashlight a little so it wasn't blinding him. "Ben? What are you doin' out there?"

He lowered his arms. "Sorry, Miz Johnson. I didn't mean to scare you. I found this knife when I was out checkin' on the fig trees I planted yesterday. Makin' sure they didn't get blown over or washed away. It was layin' on top of the rain barrel. I seen that detective's car goin' up your driveway on my way home, so I thought I'd bring it over since the rain slacked off."

"Well, don't stand there like a bump on a log. Shuck off those muddy boots and come inside."

"Why don't you just leave the knife outside, too," PC added.

He slipped his wellies off and draped his rain slicker over a rocking chair on the porch before he stepped through the door.

If that knife had been sitting out in this frog-choking rain, the odds of finding trace evidence were between slim and none, and

Slim just got out of town. Not to mention Masters getting his fingerprints all over it bringing it to Justice's. And that's assuming this was the first time he'd handled it.

PC picked up her plastic cup and got paper towels to clean up the spilled water. She didn't entirely trust Masters, even though Justice didn't seem to have a problem with him popping up out of nowhere in the dark.

"You want somethin' hot to drink, hon? Stove's gas—it should still be workin."

"No, thank you." He stayed near the door and kept his head down.

The pace of raindrops hitting the roof and windows picked up to a frenzy.

Justice shone her flashlight on one of the kitchen chairs. "May as well make yourself comfortable and wait out the storm."

A roll of thunder underlined her point.

He shuffled across the kitchen and sat. PC stayed where she could keep an eye on him, at least as well as she could do in the dark. Justice was easy to follow, because she had the flashlight. PC watched as she pulled out a stepstool and placed it in front of her refrigerator to access a small cabinet above it. The goat farmer pulled out two camp lanterns and stepped down. She turned one of them on and set it in the middle of the table.

"We'll keep this other one aside, in case anybody needs to go to the bathroom or whatever." Justice pulled out a glass from the cabinet and filled it with tap water. She set it down next to Masters.

PC could now see well enough to find the garbage can and deposited her wet paper towels inside. While Justice was putting away the stool, PC noted that the chairs were wood—and easy to clean—so she sat down at the table with Masters. His shoulders were hunched and he was picking at the skin around one thumbnail with the other thumb.

"Ben, relax, sugar. PC don't bite." Justice took the seat opposite PC, so Masters was between them.

"Sorry, Miz Johnson. I-I ran outta my medicine, and I, uh, haven't been able to get any more."

"Why didn't you say so? I would have got it for you."

"Thank you, ma'am." His leg jerked up and down, as if he were trying to tap out Morse Code with his heel.

Could he be dangerous without his meds? "What kind of medication are you on, Ben?"

"Primrose!"

"It's okay, Miz Johnson. It's buspirone. I have…I have anxiety. I'm okay on my own, but if I have to be around people too much, I get panic attacks."

"Is there anything we can do to help, hon?" Justice reached out and patted his hand.

He stiffened and she pulled the offending digits away sharply.

"Sorry," they both said, not quite in unison.

"That's why you were so nervous when Officer Tran and I were talking to you, isn't it?"

Masters nodded.

"I see. That makes sense. We're just trying to understand what happened to Dr. McIlwraith. Especially since he was found out here on Justice's place."

Masters' head jerked up. "No! She didn't do anything!"

"And how do you know that? Did you see something?"

He put his elbows on the table and leaned his head into his hands. "Yes."

Now we're getting somewhere! "Would you like to tell me what you saw?"

"Not really, but I don't want the law after Miz Johnson." He sighed. "All the trees and bushes between Miz Johnson's fence line and my house? That's my food forest. I planned it real careful. Lot a native trees and common cultivars. I always have plenty to eat and put up for the winter, but if somebody got in there and stole my food, well, nothing I could do but go hungry. I work hard to keep strangers off my place."

Was McIlwraith out there in the dark picking peaches? PC struggled to keep her mouth shut and let him talk. He rubbed his forehead. It was a good sign—he was finding his words, but she still wanted him to hurry up and spill the beans.

"I had started a fast on Wednesday. Nothin' but water for three days. Miz Johnson, I don't want you to think less of me. I know not everybody understands. But I had made myself a strong mushroom tea and I was gonna drink that and spend some time in my sweat lodge."

Justice scrunched up her face. "How is mushroom tea different from soup? Broth is broth, ain't it?"

PC cleared her throat. "Not mushrooms you can get in the grocery store."

Justice cocked her head to one side, then her eyes got wide as realization hit. "Oh! You talkin' magic mushrooms?"

Masters nodded.

"Well, at least you ain't lickin' toads."

He gave her a tiny smile. "I came out of the lodge, and there was a man standing there. "I'm fuzzy on the details. He was talking about forefathers and ancestors. I thought… well, I thought he was a vision. I was a little scared he might be an evil spirit, disguised as a teacher. He had a big silver magic wand that clicked. He told me he was looking for a key." Masters shook his head. "Not just any key. It was the key to everything. If he got a hold of that key, he'd know all the secrets. I told him I wanted to know all the secrets, too. That's why I was in the sweat lodge. He laughed at me, and I thought—oh, this is probably a bad spirit."

"And then what happened?" Justice asked, breathless.

"He was askin' me about William's cabin. I had no idea what he was talkin' about. I don't know any William. He got mad. I was sure he was a demon, come to test me. We got in a tussle. He fell, hit his head on—something. It's all kinda blurry. He wasn't movin' though. I couldn't tell if it was a trick, or he was the weakest demon in all creation. There was somethin' or somebody else, standin' just out of the firelight. I thought sure it was another demon, and I was gonna get torn all apart. Suddenly, it was mornin' and I woke up on the ground, wearin' only what God gave me. I went into the lodge nekkid, so that wasn't too big of a surprise. The fire had burned itself out, so that was a good thing."

"And where was the man?" PC asked.

Masters shrugged. "I didn't expect him to be there. Far as I knew, he was a vision. Wasn't 'til days later when I seen that archaeologist guy's picture in the paper that I thought I might be wrong about that."

"Why didn't you say somethin', hon?"

"Miz Johnson, you know as well as I do that the po-lice would have just arrested me for controlled substances. I have a right to psylocibin as part of my religion, but they tend not to see it that way. I don't know what happened to him after I passed out. He musta got up and walked off. What else coulda happened? I didn't think my vision quest tale was gonna help any."

PC tapped her index finger on the table. "What about the feral hogs?"

Justice shook her head. "Couldn't have been them. They eat everything, and I mean bones and all."

Then why didn't they eat Masters, since he was completely helpless?

PC had to consider the unpleasant possibility that either Masters was lying about what happened after Dr. McIlwraith fell, or he had no recollection of butchering the archaeologist. The hunting knife—exactly the kind used to field dress a deer—on the back porch didn't make her feel any better. What were the odds, really, that some unknown person would be wandering through random pastures at night, stumble upon two unconscious men, butcher one, and leave his bones in Justice's compost pile? That sounded even crazier than Masters' drug-enhanced vision quest story.

What if he had a psychotic break and attacked her and Justice?

The dogs started barking.

Now what? Did Masters have a partner in crime that he was waiting to arrive before he tried anything? Justice said he had friends over for drumming circles.

It could also be true that Masters was telling the truth. And the so-called 'evil spirit' might not want him to tell anyone else what had happened.

PC cast her eyes around the kitchen, looking for something that could be used as a weapon. Justice's flashlight was lightweight and plastic. There were bound to be knives—they were in a kitchen after all—but PC had no idea where they were. Her chair was unwieldy, but it was better than nothing. There. On the cooktop. A cast-iron skillet.

"I need more water. Anybody else want some?" She stood up and headed toward the sink.

Justice shook her head.

Masters picked his mostly full glass up and set it back on the table.

The detective pulled another glass from the cabinet and filled it. She stood near the stove, taking small sips of water. The pan was in easy reach, if worse came to worse.

A bright flashlight beam cut through one of the front windows and played along the shadowed corners of the kitchen.

Justice froze. Masters put his head on the table.

"Turn off the lantern!" PC hissed at Justice.

The detective grabbed the skillet and moved as fast as she could in the dark for the unlocked front door. She stood in the shadows, her heart thumping out of her chest. Surely the person on the front porch could hear it. A rivulet of sweat slid down her forehead. She struggled to keep her breath slow and silent. Careful footsteps echoed on the porch. The dogs still barked from their shelter. PC raised the frying pan.

The knob turned and the door started to ease open.

Chapter 16

THE FLASHLIGHT PRECEDED the person holding it through the front door. PC held her breath, waiting for a head to come into range.

"Ms. Johnson? PC?"

"Tran?" PC lowered the skillet.

He whirled to face her. The beam of light reflected off the pan. "Were you going to hit me with that?"

"Only if you were a killer. Why are you here?"

"Your mama called. She said you hadn't made it home and she was worried about you. I thought I'd drive out this way to make sure you weren't dead in a ditch somewhere."

Hiro Tran closed the door behind him and stepped into the living room.

PC gestured toward the kitchen. "Why didn't you just call?"

"We did. You never picked up."

The detective reached for her back pocket to find her phone. It wasn't there. "Huh. I must have left it in the car. But I'm glad you're here."

They moved into the kitchen.

Tran looked around. "Why's that?"

"Ben Masters has a story to tell you."

It was Wednesday afternoon, and the mud from the storm three days ago hadn't even dried yet. But the orthopedic surgeon's office in Houston was cool and, if they were close to a window, sunny.

Rose walked across the exam room without her cane or a walker.

Dr. Thompson nodded. "That looks great, Rose. The lift fits you perfectly. How do you feel about it?"

"It sure did help. The pain I was havin' went away almost overnight. I feel like I'm almost as good as I was before I fell."

The doctor scooped up her chart. "Unless you start having any pain or feel like the joint is wobbly, I don't need to see you again until January. That'll be the one-year post-surgery checkup."

Is that it then? Can I go back to Houston? Will Rocky be able to help out enough that I can leave? The gate to the corral that was holding her in Possumwood had started to crack open. Did she make a run for it now, or wait until it swung all the way?

PC made her mother's appointment, and they were halfway to Brandee's when Rose's phone rang.

"Rocky? Everything okay?…Sure…Okay…We're still probably 45 minutes or so out, though…See you then."

"What's going on?"

Rose chewed her lip as she put her phone away. "He wouldn't say. Just wants us to meet him at the Brisk Rib as soon as we get to Possumwood."

"Huh." *What could this be about? If he'd decided to skip town, he'd probably have just slunk off without telling anybody.* "You don't need a pit stop, do you?"

"No. I just wanna know what's goin' on with your brother."

Me, too, Mama. Me, too. "Did he sound happy? Upset?"

"Neither."

"Wonder if he's invited Daisy."

"He didn't say. She's got her hands full with Zach's graduation next week, though."

PC set the cruise control at a little faster than the speed limit. "What could it be? He's lost his job? He's found a girlfriend? He won the lotto?"

Rose shrugged. "I guess we'll just have to wait."

The detective exited the freeway and took Farm to Market 999. Soon, ribbony leaves of young rice plants shimmied in the breeze to their left. Fluffy white Charolais cattle dotted a spring-green pasture to their right. The dark asphalt snaked across the prairie beneath them, then the land gave way to gently rolling hills.

"You wanna text Rocky and tell him we're almost there?"

Rose retrieved her phone from her oversized purse. "Hello, Rocky?…Just hit the Mirabella County line…I think so. About fifteen minutes…Bye, honey."

"Any clues?"

"No."

As they got closer to the Brisk Rib, butterflies beat their wings against PC's stomach. *What has Rocky got to say? Good news? Bad? He could at least have told us that.*

PC pulled into a parking slot next to the front door. The lunch crowd had long disappeared. Rocky was easy to spot—he sat at the only occupied table in the place, facing them. Someone was with him, but she wasn't sure who it was, based on the back of their head. Was it Rocky's boss, Durelle Fennec? *Oh, dear.*

Rose passed her daughter and headed toward the cashier. "He said it'd probably be a good idea to go ahead and get some lunch."

PC followed, unsure if she could eat.

It felt like it took three hours to get their food and drinks. Rose shuffled along the concrete floor toward Rocky's table. He got up and met her, taking the tray.

PC hoped her voice didn't quiver. "Hey, Rocky. Ms. Fennec. What's going on?"

"We really need to talk about Rocky's future." Durelle Fennec took a swig of her tea.

Rose plopped down in her chair and PC winced. *Don't break your other hip, Mama.* She took the remaining chair.

"Is he getting fired?" Rose fidgeted with her napkin.

"No. Course not! That did sound kinda ominous, didn't it? Sorry 'bout that."

PC picked up her fork, and Rose flattened the napkin in her lap.

Durelle continued. "I need more skilled labor. I'm not gonna lie. There already aren't enough qualified workers in patient care, and who's gonna come to Possumwood, anyway, when they could make a lot more money in the big city?"

Rose pushed her coleslaw around on her plate. PC started in on her potato.

"Miz Fennec asked me this mornin' if I was interested in becomin' a CNA. That's a Certified Nursin' Assistant."

"I found a grant for a CNA program in Spring that Rocky's eligible for. He can work part time and go to school part time. It's a three-month program. But it's very challenging, and he's really gonna need your support. I wanted to make sure you were fully on board before I applied for the grant."

Rose finally let out the breath she'd apparently been holding. "That's great! But aren't we just about outta spring?" She took a bite of her brisket.

"Spring, Texas. You know. North of Houston."

"When does it start?" Rose scooped some barbeque onto her fork.

"First Monday in June."

PC sipped her tea. "And this is something you really want to do?"

Rocky sucked his teeth, as if trying to interpret his sister's question. "I know it took a while to get my GED after I dropped outta high school. But this is different. I can be more than some drunk bum. This is a chance to help other people while I'm also helpin' myself."

"I never expected to see you in the medical field, that's all." *Rocky, please stick with it this time.* PC tried to hide her doubt with a half-smile.

"You may even end up bein' a doctor, when it's all said and done!" Rose waved her sauce-covered fork towards her son.

"I don't know about that, Mama. Let me just get this CNA done first, okay?"

Rose beamed and scooped up some coleslaw.

PC looked into Rocky's eyes. "If it's really what you want to do, I'll support you any way I can. But you're not practicing drawing blood on me, got it? No needles."

He laughed.

Durelle put both her hands flat on the table and pushed her chair back. "I really wanted to make sure y'all were on board with this. It's gonna be a lotta stress on your family while he's goin' to school. It'll be late nights when he's in class, and I worry about you being all by yourself. I know you've been havin' your own health troubles, Rose. I didn't want to egg him on if it was gonna be too much of a strain on you."

"Thank you for keepin' me in mind, Durelle. We'll be just fine. I got Primrose here to help keep me goin.'"

"It's decided then?" Rocky's boss paused for anyone to speak or forever hold their peace. "I'll go back to my office and get the paperwork submitted. It's all ready to go. Just have to press send." She stood and picked up her purse.

"Thank you, honey. It means so much to me that Rocky's got somebody else looking out for him." Rose's eyelashes glistened with unshed tears.

The nursing home director smiled and gave Rose's shoulder a squeeze before she walked out the door.

PC finished her potato while Rose and Rocky jabbered excitedly. She was happy for her brother's opportunity. He wasn't always known for his stick-to-itiveness, but she hoped this time was an exception. He needed this. Rose needed this. PC could hear the echo of that corral gate slamming shut, though. There was no way Rocky could go to school *and* take care of their mother's menagerie. Rose might be able to start doing some of it, but it was hard work, and the last thing anybody needed was for her to fall and break her other hip.

Speaking of lost souls... "Rocky? Could you run Mama home when she's done eating? Since we're right here, I wanted to run into the station and check on some things."

"Sure thing."

"Thanks, Rocky. See you in a little bit, Mama."

PC cleared her dishes and walked the two blocks to Possum-wood PD. Annie buzzed her in and the detective found Tran in his cubicle.

"PC. I was gonna text you. I had a question about the incident at Ms. Johnson's place."

"What's that?"

"You said that Ben Masters had a hunting knife that he left on the back porch. Did you put it somewhere?"

"No."

"We couldn't locate it. I thought you'd put it out of reach or something when Masters was there."

"He said he found it and was bringing it to me." PC shrugged. "Maybe it slipped through the gap between the boards on the deck? Or maybe he could have changed his mind and gone back for it after he made bail."

"He didn't. He's still in lockup."

PC felt an iceberg calve into the pit of her stomach. "What if that shadowy figure wasn't imaginary after all?" *Had he been at Justice's lurking outside during the storm? And did Masters know?*

Tran raised an eyebrow. "Masters admitted to struggling with McIlwraith. He was under the influence of psychoactive substances and doesn't have a clue what happened after the archaeologist hit his head. At least, that's what he says. There was nobody else out there."

PC frowned.

"You don't look convinced."

"In two and a half decades, I've seen a lot of crazy things caused by people taking drugs. But not shrooms. If he'd said K2, that'd be totally different."

"K2?"

"Synthetic cannabis. People go completely insane on that stuff."

Tran nodded. "You caught the killer. Call it a day."

"Are the Rangers still coming out on Friday?"

"Not sure." Tran turned and tapped the enter key on his laptop to keep it from going into sleep mode.

"I canceled them." Woody paused on his way from the break room, a steaming cup of black coffee in his hand. "We have his confession. It's up to the DA and the jury now."

The detective bit her tongue. *How could he confess, if he didn't remember what happened?*

The smell of the java made PC crave her own cup. Woody's cheekbones seemed more angular than normal this afternoon. "Have you lost weight, Chief?"

"You aren't planning on attending Settler's Day next month, are you Donovan?"

"Why do you ask?"

"Just trying to decide if I should order more body bags."

"Standup comedy is tough. Don't quit your day job."

He grinned and headed back to his office, clearly believing he got under her skin.

Look out Settler's Day. Here I come! Nobody die this time, alright?

If you enjoyed this book, please consider leaving a review at your favorite book site. Reviews help other readers find and enjoy new books!

Other books by Holly Dey:

Manor of Death: The Possumwood Mysteries Book 1

Death on the Half Shell: The Possumwood Mysteries Book 2

Azalea Trail of Death: The Possumwood Mysteries Book 3

Death Re-Enacted: The Possumwood Mysteries Book 4

Death Rides a Bobcat: The Possumwood Mysteries Book 5

Key to Death: The Possumwood Mysteries Book 6

Death Curated: The Possumwood Mysteries Book 7

Pool of Death: The Possumwood Mysteries Book 8

All Death No Cattle: The Possumwood Mysteries Book 9

Death is Lager than Life: The Possumwood Mysteries Book 10

Art of Death: The Possumwood Mysteries Book 11

Little Town of Death-Lehem: The Possumwood Mysteries Book 12

Winter: Boxset Collection Books 1-3

Spring: Boxset Collection Books 4-6

Summer: Boxset Collection Books 7-9

Fall: Boxset Collection Books 10-12

All of the Possumwood Mysteries are available in

Large Print Editions

Other books by Holly Day